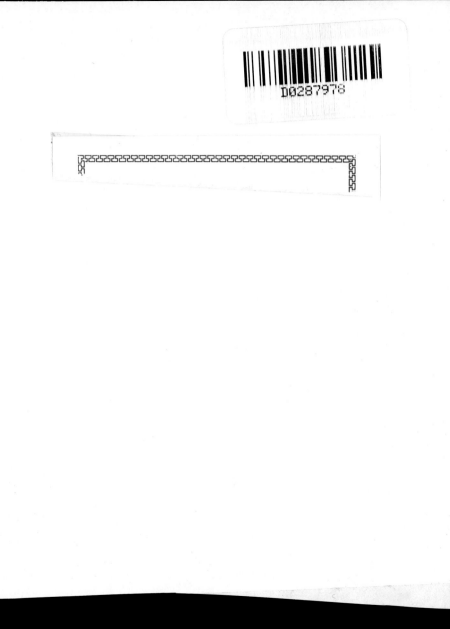

OLD
WARS

David Helwig

VIKING

VIKING
Published by the Penguin Group
Penguin Books Canada Ltd, 2801 John Street, Markham,
Ontario, Canada L3R 1B4
Penguin Books Ltd, 27 Wrights Lane, London W8 5TZ,
England
Viking Penguin Inc., 40 West 23rd Street, New York, New York
10010, USA
Penguin Books Australia Ltd, Ringwood, Victoria, Australia
Penguin Books (NZ) Ltd, 182-190 Wairau Road, Auckland 10,
New Zealand

Penguin Books Ltd, Registered Offices: Harmondsworth,
Middlesex, England

First published 1989
1 3 5 7 9 10 8 6 4 2

Printed and bound in Canada

Canadian Cataloguing in Publication Data
Helwig, David, 1938-
Old wars

ISBN 0-670-82593-X

I. Title.

PS8515.E58054 1989   C813'.54   C88-094758-6
PR9199.3.H45054 1989

American Library of Congress Cataloguing in Publication Data
V82593-X   OLD WARS   88-51905

OLD
WARS

1

*I*t was something in the quality of the silence as he approached the house that made him turn and run, and
from the first second his concentration was on the stone
cairn. The decision to run, the first steps, and the echoing
noise of the rifles all came together, and the sequence of
events was confused. He knew the shots were coming from
inside the house, and then he was hit, sky and earth were
spinning, and he lost his sense of direction, though still the
cairn was part of what he saw as he fell. It was only after he
was down that he knew he had got far enough to knock it
over. Nick wouldn't blunder into a trap.

It was after he had fallen that the pain became sharp, and
then vivid as the blue Mediterranean sky and sea, and
finally so intense that he was aware of nothing else, except
the sky pressing down on him and making the pain spread.
Then he saw the uniforms, and they were carrying him into
the house.

It was strange, human, almost comforting to be touched by
the hands of the men carrying him, even though they had
shot him and would, now or later, kill him. Still, at this mo-

ment they were holding him, and their human hands seemed to mute the screaming of the pain.

He wondered if they would realize the importance of the stone cairn and try to rebuild it. He couldn't understand German, but he tried to concentrate on the rhythm of their speech, the quality of sound, to know if they were concerned about it.

Inside the house, the suitcase containing the radio was open. They would try to get him to play back false information.

When he refused to do that, they would kill him.

It was not long until Nick was due back. If he saw the cairn down, he would stop before he came in sight of the house. Nick would escape. Perhaps even come and save him.

No, that was impossible, and Nick had little use for him anyway.

In Nick's war, he was part of the enemy.

The Germans were tying his hands and gagging his mouth.

He prepared himself to die.

2

He no longer noticed that he was waiting. At one time anticipation, patient or impatient, had been at the front of his consciousness, then later barely out of sight, as if around a corner of his awareness, ominous and secret, but always present. Now it was like some kind of intuitive knowledge that altered the texture of every moment without being a conscious part of any one of them. It was a fact that he didn't mention to himself.

There was an ache in his leg as he drove through the half-dark of early morning, and he told himself he should have stayed in bed longer, but knew that was wrong, that when sleep left him in the early hours he might as well get up and be busy. Still, if he finished too soon at the church, it would leave empty hours to be filled. He was careful not to do that, to lay out the day in such a way that it had a pattern, a place for everything, no surprises. He didn't want to look too closely behind him or in front.

The sky was gradually lighter in the east, and the

heater was taking the chill off the car. Perhaps when it got warm, his leg would stop aching, though he didn't count on it.

There were several strange cars at the motel, hunters likely. In the afternoon, he might go out past the pond and see if he could find a duck or a partridge. It would be so easy to put the gun away, even sell it, one more act of retirement, the slow process of retraction by which you detached one connection after another from the world and sank down into yourself to wait for death. He pulled into the drive at the side of the church.

In the last few minutes, the light had spread in the grey sky until now it was as bright as it would get on this overcast November morning. As he climbed from the car, he shivered and yawned. Why wasn't he home in bed? There wasn't more than a half-day's work at the church; he could have started at noon. He unlocked the door and went in.

He tried to analyse his own reaction to the church building sometimes. Mostly, it seemed something connected with Jean and therefore warm, decent, lovable. He had never attended with her, and her funeral had been strange, as if she were giving a party for her friends to which he wasn't invited. She belonged there. He didn't.

But now he did, in his own way. The subject had come up at the funeral, that the former janitor was ill and having to give up the work.

Had Tom Barclay mentioned it on purpose? Not likely. Jean's friends thought Malcolm out of place, even now, as the caretaker of the building. In summer as he mowed the lawn, church members were especially careful to be friendly to him when they passed. They didn't want to seem snobs, but they were uneasy that Jean's husband had taken on this menial work.

He got the vacuum out of the closet and carried it to the chancel. Would Margaret appear this morning? Every day he had a little bet with himself about whether she would appear, and most days she did. She was a tall awkward woman who came to pray or talk or only sit and watch him, and once a week to wax the wood and polish the brass in the sanctuary. Tom Barclay had explained at the beginning that Margaret would do that. It was a task that she had taken on years before, and she clung to it. Almost every day, she spent some time in the church. She too was alone and needed ways to fill the time. She seemed to be coming earlier recently, and the first thing she did was to use the toilet. He suspected that there was something wrong with hers that she was too poor or shy to have fixed, and once or twice he had suggested that if she had trouble with anything at her house and needed a handyman he would be glad to help.

Did they pay her for her attention to the sanctuary? He thought not; her clothes looked as if she could use the money. She didn't work and wasn't married; what did she live on? His own poverty had made him sensitive to the poverty of others. Just how badly off was she? He could ask Tom Barclay, but it would seem merely intrusive to want to know such things about her.

He worked at a steady pace, trying to avoid positions that would increase the pains in his leg. He tired more quickly now. What would happen when he could no longer do the cleaning here? He would have to live on the small pension and cut out his few luxuries, Scotch, newspapers. If prices got too high, he would have to sell his house and get a small apartment.

Once, as he was vacuuming, he thought someone was watching him, and he turned quickly to see if Margaret had come in the front door. There was no one. It was an atavism, this prickling at the back of the neck, the third eye and third ear picking up warnings. The pure animal instinct to survive that could perceive unheard sounds. He looked toward the chancel where the stained-glass windows over the altar brightened as a moment of sunlight passed over them.

Why was the instinct for danger coming back? Was it death he was being warned about, the body picking up the earliest signals from its own chemistry? He had never been old before and could have no idea what complex betrayals were possible. Once he would have known what to do about the warnings, no, that was to falsify, one never knew what to do, but once he would have trusted the signals and begun a process of seeking their source.

He changed positions and moved the vacuum nozzle with one hand. If he stayed in one position for too long, his back began to stiffen. When he finished this part of the church, he would stop and make coffee and eat the sandwich he had put in his jacket pocket. He preferred having breakfast when he was thoroughly awake.

Was it the measure of his loneliness that he was anticipating Margaret's arrival almost impatiently? If he had met the woman a few years ago, he would have thought of her simply as an eccentric old maid and ignored her. Now he found that he was observing her peculiarities with something that was almost affection. He spent time wondering about the old stuffed chair on her porch, why she left it out there in the weather. What prompted her to wear a pair of blue jeans that were too short for her long legs? Did she get her clothes second-hand?

His world was growing emptier, Jean dead, Edward settled in Vancouver with his wife and two children. He only heard from them at Christmas. He had thought of inviting his grandson Frank to come and spend some time with him in the summer, was still considering it. Would the boy be embarrassed at finding his grandfather was a janitor? Edward had been shocked and displeased when he heard. He wouldn't want it known among the other accountants. Odd, the symbolism of certain jobs. The man who came to clean out the septic tanks didn't smell, the big suction hose on his truck did all the work, but still he made self-conscious jokes about his business.

Edward had always been too self-possessed, proper and censorious. Where had that come from? Perhaps he had created it. He and Jean had married just after the war when he met her in Ottawa, and Edward was born a couple of years later. It was a time when he had needed everything to be proper, controlled.

But Jean's warmth had made it good. Edward had no warmth.

The rug by the church door was full of mud and stones and leaves that had blown in when the door was opened. The vacuum wasn't doing much of a job of picking up the dirt. He checked the bag. Which was full.

He had been trained for this job by the housework he had done in the years after his retirement. Jean, who was twelve years younger than he was, was still working several days a week at the travel agency, so it had seemed only fair for him to do the housework since he was at home all day. When he had first started, he had been awkward and inexpert, and Jean had been uncomfortable about it, but he had persisted, and soon it all worked smoothly. They had a pleasant life, too pleasant perhaps. The fates had observed them and reached their angry fingers into Jean's body and torn her apart. By the time they phoned him from the hospital, she was dead. He had been reading a newspaper and planning supper. She had been late for work that morning, had kissed him quickly on the cheek as she ran to the door. He had never seen her alive again.

As he walked through the church with the new bag for the vacuum, his eyes moved over the brass memorial plaques. *In Loving Memory of James Pearson Coulthart.* In the church hall there was one from 1910 in memory of a boy who had drowned while trying to rescue two companions.

He put the bag in the vacuum, then stood still, listening. A car had stopped nearby. That was of no significance. Why was he listening like this?

He was afraid that it was the beginning of senility, certain old habits, old reactions reasserting themselves. He hoped that the nightmares didn't come back. It was Jean who saw him through them before.

They had met, become engaged, married so quickly, with such a sense of joyful urgency that he hadn't told her about the nightmares, the insomnia, until one night a few weeks before the wedding when Jean made it clear that she expected to stay at his apartment. He was pleased and then suddenly embarrassed. It would frighten her if he woke thrashing around. He started to explain.

"I hadn't intended to let you sleep much," she said, kissing him. That had startled him, for she was a virgin and he had expected her to be skittish or at least tentative.

He had loved her deeply till the day of her death. It was so terribly unfair to them both, that sudden, early, unforeseen death. Women of fifty-six didn't have heart attacks.

He thought of stopping and making coffee now, but decided to finish the vacuuming as he'd planned. Systematic. Was he that by nature or was it the police work that had bred it in him?

He had finished cleaning the church and was in the little kitchen making coffee when he heard, or sensed, that Margaret had entered the side door of the church hall. In a few minutes he would hear the flush of the toilet. He sat down with his coffee and the cheese sandwich. Usually she went from the toilet to the church where she knelt in prayer. Later she might speak to him.

To his surprise, after he heard the flush of the toilet, he heard Margaret's footsteps coming toward the kitchen.

David Helwig

"Who is that man, Malcolm?" she said abruptly.

"What man?"

"The one sitting just down the street in a car."

Why did he keep his face deliberately blank as he answered her? Another atavism?

"It could be anyone. Perhaps his wife is visiting nearby. Or a salesman waiting for an appointment."

"I think you should go out and send him away."

"Do you think he's up to something?"

"Yes."

"I'll go and take a look."

Margaret wasn't usually suspicious. He tried to watch her eyes as he spoke to her, but she kept her face turned away. He took a sip of his coffee.

When he got outside, there was no car parked anywhere near the church. The day was still grey and dark, but a wind was coming up and blowing leaves back on the lawn which he had raked last week. Perhaps he would do it again this afternoon.

"No one there," he told Margaret when he got back inside.

"I suppose I frightened him off."

"How?"

"Gave him my basilisk stare."

"He may have been perfectly innocent."

"I think not."

He refused to believe that she was right, after all these years.

"Why do you use the toilet here?" he said. The only way to be sure of an answer was to be blunt.

"Self-indulgence."

"What?"

"It's warmer," she said and turned and walked into

the church. Below the too-short denim jeans he could see a pair of pink socks. On her feet she wore old-fashioned laced Oxfords. He didn't think they were sold any more.

She also wore a heavy cardigan, out at the elbows, and her hair was unbrushed. She didn't look like a pious spinster, but she came every day and prayed with what seemed like intense concentration.

While she was in the church at her devotions, he swept and mopped the floor of the hall, then went back in to dust. What was the source of Margaret's intuition about the man? Was she the sort of person whose intuitions could be trusted? The instincts and knowledge of the past told him that she was, that the unconventional element in her made her more aware rather than less.

If they had come back, why now? During the years in business when he had struggled to make something of the agency for prefab houses and cottages, and later when he sold building supplies, he had been conscious every day that someone might arrive. Some days the face of every customer held a secret message. Hank Regehr, the other salesman, would notice the days when it was worst and ask if he had fought with Jean that morning. Sometimes he would let Hank think that, though it wasn't true. He couldn't imagine fighting with Jean. He owed her too much. Days when one or the other was out of sorts, they kept to themselves.

She was gone. It was wrong. It was unfair.

As he was raking the lawn, Margaret came out of the church door and looked toward him. Behind her was Rhoda Maynard's white clapboard house. To one side a large bare tree and behind that the cloudy sky, grey moving on grey. At this time of year, it seemed as if it never got fully light. Even noon was touched by darkness.

Margaret stood still, looking at him. There was a look of concern on her face.

"Don't look so worried," he said to her, loud enough for his voice to be heard over the wind. She gave an awkward wave of her hand, turned and walked away.

The wind flapped a loose edge of her cardigan.

He liked Margaret. She gave him someone to worry about. Was she serious about the toilet being warmer? What kind of heat did she have, and could she afford oil? The prices were becoming absurd; he used his oil furnace only to keep the pipes from freezing in the coldest weather. For comfort he burned wood, though that was one more thing to concern him about age and weakness. How long could he go on cutting and splitting his wood? Even when Jean was alive, she had fretted about the tree he was eventually going to drop on himself. He was skilful and careful, but the more trees you cut, the greater was the chance that one of them would misbehave and catch you off guard.

Don't borrow trouble. He had enough wood in for this winter. The next would come when it did.

His leg was aching more now, the old badly mended break.

One of the first things Jean had ever said to him. Why do you limp? Most people didn't notice it, it was such a slight inhibition in his pace, but she had spotted it right away. The sharpness of the eyes of love. That was her explanation.

He filled two plastic garbage bags with the leaves he had raked and left them by the back wall of the church hall beside the box he had built to hold the garbage cans.

On his way home in the afternoon, he stopped in town and bought a loaf of bread. Marge Powley at the cash counter told him it was a windy day, and he agreed. She told him it had been a warm fall.

"Yes, it has."

He wondered if her husband was on or off the wagon this week, but didn't ask. Since Jean's death, he found that he was out of date with local gossip of the sort that she had picked up quite regularly just by sitting at her desk and doing her work. Jean had always been his instrument of communication with others in town. She was better at dealing with people than he would ever be. He needed a framework, a business relationship or something of the sort. Jean, by the time she left the store, would have known, whether she wanted to or not, if Bert Powley was drinking. People told her things.

He drove up the hill past the two mobile homes with their flocks of children. The trees grew close to the road here, and they had cleared only enough space to set up the trailers on concrete blocks with a small drive beside for the car. The town council kept threatening to force them out, but nothing was done.

As he turned at the top of the hill, he saw a car in front of him. It hadn't been there a mile back, and judging from its speed it must have come out of his driveway. It disappeared around the curve in the road on the far side of the house. Was it the man Margaret had seen at the church? He stopped at the end of the drive and looked ahead of him up to the house. It looked perfectly normal, a small plain house, its proportions suggesting the architecture of the fifties. It was one of the prefabs he had spent four years trying to sell between Ottawa and Kingston. He had struggled to make a living at it, and had been able to get the units and build this house comparatively cheaply. It was shortly after the house was up that he gave up on the prefab agency and went to work for Charlie McLaren. A couple of years later, when Edward was twelve, Jean started to work part-time. It was only then that they were able to stop worrying about money. Sometimes, in the poor days, he knew that Jean was wondering why he had left a promising career in the RCMP for this precarious life.

Had someone been exploring his house?

He looked around, but he could see no proof that anyone had been there. The drive was too worn to show tire tracks.

Walking into the house was always a bad moment, with the painful reiteration of her absence announced by the particular silence of a house that had been uninhabited since he had left it. The cold in here made him shiver, and he wondered about lighting a fire. Or waiting till later after he came back from his hunt through the bush behind the house. He checked his watch. Just over three hours from now till dark. The best time to hunt was probably the hour before dark when he was most likely to find partridge settled in trees for the night. He wasn't a sport hunter and had no impulse to shoot birds on the wing. He was perfectly happy to pick them out of trees with a .22. He didn't understand inventing rules to make the game fairer. If you were going to kill something, you might as well kill it as quickly and efficiently as possible.

He decided to make a bowl of soup and some toast, then have a nap and get up in time to hunt for an hour before dark. He'd light a fire when he came back in.

As he opened a can of soup and put it on the stove, he saw Jean's picture watching him from the side table in the living room. The week after her death he had put that picture away, feeling that he couldn't bear to see it, but a day later he had got it out. He was damned if he would deal with his grief by trying to forget her or avoid the thought of her death. He would stare the facts in the face until they were bearable. That was his way.

He woke from the nap knowing he had just escaped from a frightening, oppressive dream, but the details disappeared on the moment of waking and left only the oppression. He folded the blankets. He filled the kettle and while it was heating, he put on a pair of work boots, took down and loaded his rifle. His arm and shoulder were stiff, and he grew angry at the difficulty he had pushing the bullets into the clip. He put the rifle by the back door, made tea with a bag in a cup and drank about half of it scalding hot before putting on an old jacket and setting out.

He walked past the garden and turned up the path into the woods. A hundred feet further on, there was an old logging road which he used for bringing out firewood, but over the years the path had developed as a kind of short cut when he was on foot. It led up the hill and down to the beaver pond on the other side. It was a little late in the year to find ducks on the pond, but it was always possible, so he walked slowly and quietly up the path to the tip of the hill and stood looking down at the pond watching for any movement. It was still except for a few ripples of wind over the surface of the water.

He moved slowly down the hill, stopping every few feet to scan the surface of the pond. His eyes were still good, though he was beginning to develop the farsightedness of age and couldn't read without glasses, but he could see every detail of the pond, the dead grey trunks of the trees that had died when the beavers flooded the area, the thickly intertwined bare branches and the brown and grey surface of the hill on the other side, the dark brown of rotting leaves and soil, the lighter brown of the newly fallen leaves.

There was nothing on the pond. He walked on down to the edge and then left to go round it and up the hill on the other side. Two or three young beech trees lay where the beavers had felled them earlier in the fall. They had felled or killed everything close to the pond and were starting to move to trees further away. Now and then he was tempted to rip out their dam to try to get rid of them, but he always decided against it.

Along the far side, there was a series of maples cut by the beavers; each lay with the butt-end on land, the upper end tangled in the dead branches over the pond or lying in the pond itself. A few of them he had hauled ashore and cut up to burn, but others were too inextricably tangled to bring down without danger or had rotted from lying in the water.

He walked up the hill beside a little freshet that was the main source of the pond's water.

As he reached the top, he heard the whirr of wings as a grouse flew off from beside him. He watched its flight through the bare branches of the trees. There was no hope of hitting it in the air with a rifle, but if he had an idea where it landed he could probably stalk it. It disappeared just over the top of the hill.

Before he moved off, he looked carefully to his right at the point where the bird had been. They sometimes fed in small groups, but there was no sign of anything there, though he knew how hard it was to see their speckled feathers against a background of leaves and twigs. The camouflage was almost perfect. He examined the ground almost inch by inch before he moved, and yet, as soon as he took a step, there was another explosion of sound and a bird flew up and off in another direction.

The hill was steep here, and near the top he had to stop and catch his breath. As he stood, he calculated where the first of the birds might have landed. He turned and angled a bit to the right so that the area would come into his field of vision a little more quickly.

The wind had fallen now, and the clouds had opened so that the setting sun was shining across the trees. He saw a dark shape on one of the branches. It was the partridge. Slowly and silently he lifted the rifle to his shoulder. It had only an open sight, but when he had first bought the gun he had tested it and filed the front and back sights carefully to a point

that allowed him to shoot with precision. The bird
was just under a hundred feet away. At that distance
he didn't have to expect any drop in the bullet; he
had filed the sights to be accurate at a hundred feet.
He set the sights on the small target of the bird's head
and took the first pressure on the trigger. The ache
in his shoulder made it hard to hold the gun steady,
but he concentrated on the steady aim of the gun and
the pain seemed to subside.

The loud fast crack of the rifle echoed through the
trees and the bird flopped to the ground, thrashed
for a second and lay still. By the time he reached it, it
seemed quite dead, but he snapped the neck and
then quickly began to pluck it while the body was
warm and the feathers loose. The mottled feathers
had a beautiful pattern of brown and black and
white.

By the time he was done, it was almost dark and
suddenly colder. He felt a slight chill as he stood up,
stretched his stiff back and turned toward the house.
He emptied the cartridges from the gun and put
them in his pocket, then walked with the bird dan-
gling from one hand, the gun in the other.

For the first time, he allowed himself to think of
the car that seemed to have come from his driveway.
He went back over the moment in his mind, trying to
define the exact second he had caught a glimpse of
the car and where it was. On the road, but still partly
in the wrong lane as if it had pulled out and was just
turning into the far lane to drive away.

It had been coming out of his driveway.

It was almost dark as he walked down the hill to the
beaver pond. The water had a dark silver shimmer

and the trees were black twisted shapes. He was cold now and tired and full of aches, and he was alone in the world by the edge of this silver water, standing still for a moment to breathe in the cold air.

3

The plane came down into the space between the dark clouds and the dark earth. Below, the countryside near Ottawa was a pattern of black and hard grey and dim green and a range of winter browns. It seemed to Borden Denny that he had left behind too much, sunlight and too much else. Perhaps it was only the hangover. Bud Hurnick had taken him out the night before and filled him with Jack Daniel's by way of farewell, and his head felt swollen and aching.

But it was more than that. The trip from Washington to Ottawa was a slide from the big world to a smaller one. They hadn't shown him everything at Langley; they couldn't, but even what they had made available left him feeling like a country cousin. The satellite photographs scanned by computer with anomalies instantly recorded and signalled to the desks of duty officers. The speed and sophistication of document analysis. The sheer size and complexity of the operation.

21

The plane was passing over a patch of bare wood-
land as they lost altitude and approached the airport.
The trees were black and spindly, and the day
seemed even darker than it had a moment before.
When the plane took off from Washington, the sun
had been shining, and he had seen the suburbs roll-
ing underneath hm, a busy miniature world that he
watched over like a god. But then they had risen to
cruising altitude and the earth had vanished in cloud,
and the drink he had bought had only made the
heaviness of his head worse, as if the cloud and darkness had got inside it.

They bumped down on the runway. All the bodies
on the plane rose and began to claim coats and bags.
Borden hated being caught in slow-moving crowds
like this, little imprisoned steps gradually drawing
you along the aisle so that once you broke free you
wanted to run.

Would the immigration officer ask the purpose of
his trip? Consultations on parole procedures. That
was the explanation to be given. He was still officially
attached to the parole service, his real job not identified for reasons of security and because the service
he worked for didn't officially exist. The decision had
been made in principle to replace the RCMP with a
civilian security service, but the legislation hadn't yet
passed through Parliament, and while all that was going on it was best not to have too much obvious activ-
ity. Journalists were like a nest of bees once you
stirred them up; best to calm them with honey, stun
them with smoke. It was generally assumed that the
RCMP Security Service was still operating, and that
was true, but within the Solicitor-General's Depart-

ment, under the Planning and Analysis Branch, there was a gradual building program going on, in silence.

In the first interview, it had taken Borden a few nervous minutes to understand what was happening. He'd thought at first that he had blotted his copybook somehow and the men in front of him were considering whether his government appointment should be terminated. They were all strangers to him, and unduly severe. Their early questions were about his attitude to his work and the prison and parole systems; then suddenly they shifted to his undergraduate record, the courses in history and politics. It was then he caught on, and he wondered, as he gave perfectly true answers, how they could have known that these answers, which anyone with any brains knew to be the right ones, were sincere. They should, he thought, use a polygraph; not that it was infallible, but the readings would give them a further basis for analysis, even for questioning. If you wanted to know a man well, it would be useful to query him on polygraph anomalies. His explanations would give you a good sense of how fully he knew himself, and that, after all, was the central piece of information about anyone who would be dealing in a secret world.

The Americans had been sympathetic to his problems; he had to represent a non-existent agency, attempting to work without rules, with the RCMP possessive and demoralized, the few new people lacking clear responsibility. They had given him as much information as they reasonably could, even a tip on something that might be worth looking into over the next few weeks. Bud Hurnick had mentioned it unofficially one night when they were in his apartment listening to records. He collected old 78s, especially country and western, and he had just picked up a couple of early Hank Snow songs. Bud had a huge collection of 78s, and because they were so heavy he'd had a special mahogany cabinet made for them. He'd been hearing rumours that he might be transferred abroad — there were a couple of people they had to get out of Guatemala — and he was concerned about leaving his apartment empty.

"You could give it up," Borden had said. "Put everything in storage."

"No." Bud shook his head. "You got to have a place to come back to. You got to know what you're defending, what you're fighting for. You got to be able to think about home."

Borden rode downtown on the airport bus, got off in front of the Lord Elgin and set out to walk to his apartment. His cases were heavy, but he needed the exercise and fresh air. When he got unpacked he would phone Cynthia and they would meet for dinner.

Like the whole city, his apartment was dark and small. The building superintendent had left a pile of mail on the kitchen table, but none of it was of much interest. He threw most of it into the waste basket. Then unpacked, put the dirty clothes in a bag to be washed, and took a shower.

Out of the shower, he stood naked by the apartment window and looked out over the city, the hotels of the downtown where delegations and lobbyists sought favour, the corner of the West Block of the parliament buildings, the dark stone and Gothic design offering a Victorian image of significance. It wasn't like Washington with its classic eighteenth-century buildings surrounded by squalor; Ottawa didn't have the excitement, the verve, the sense of danger. In the distance, he could see the Gatineau Hills. They were on the edge of the forest, the edge of darkness. The cars were turning on their lights. He wondered if the Russians felt more at home here. It was always twilight in Ottawa. The average January temperature in Ottawa was a degree or two colder than the average in Moscow. Perhaps the Russians hated it because it was like home.

Naked, reborn after the trip to Washington, he faced the city and its secrets. He was to be one of the new masters of the secret world. He'd always enjoyed the irony of knowing more than others. Growing up, he had been so surrounded by eyes, his parents, older sister, younger sister, that it had been one of his chief luxuries to keep things to himself. He'd told the interrogators that, in the second interview when it had become explicit what they were offering him, and when they had asked about his ability to keep his mouth shut.

He met Cynthia for dinner at Mamma Teresa's. She seemed preoccupied, the perfect doll-like face turning away from him too often, as if she were searching the restaurant for someone else who might be there, as if, in the candlelight, someone might be observing her. Borden wondered if he was becoming too suspicious, searching too hard for some kind of inner meaning to everything, but when they got back to her apartment, and after they had made love, she told him that she was breaking it off.

"Why?" Borden said. "Is there someone else?"

"Yes."

"I wasn't away long. You got lonely in a hurry."

"I knew before you went away."

He had climbed from bed and was looking back toward her. Her cheeks were bright pink, her eyes a clear blue under the thin arched line of the brows. Perfect white teeth. There was nothing about the face to offset the delicate china-doll beauty, but her body, as she sat up on the edge of the bed, was thin, almost awkward. She had high shoulders, narrow, pointed breasts. Borden watched her, wondering what she was feeling. He wondered what he was feeling.

"So this," he said, with a gesture toward the bed, "was just to say goodbye."

"I guess."

He went and knelt in front of her. He put his hands over her breasts which vanished behind his broad palms. He moved them in slow circles.

"Borden . . . no . . ."

"Why not?"

"It's over."

"When was it over? The moment I came? Ten seconds after?"

"It was over when I told you."

"You want to make all the rules."

He pushed her back on the bed. She didn't resist, but there were tears in her eyes. He continued to touch her body, stimulating her, listening to her draw in her breath.

"Who is he?"

"It doesn't matter, does it? You don't know him."

"What does he have that I don't?"

He moved on top and went inside her. She sighed, but didn't speak.

"What does he have that I don't?" he repeated.

"A heart," she said.

She was trying not to respond, but her body betrayed her. Borden moved carefully, slowly, gently, brought her to orgasm once, then again. His own orgasm was very intense, left him breathless.

They lay side by side in the bed, and he reached out and touched her hair.

"You had to do that, didn't you?" she said. "You had to be in control."

"And he doesn't?"

"No."

"Not yet."

He rose from the bed and reached for his clothes. Two months ago, he might have been frightened to be going away from her, to know he wouldn't see her again, but when he was in Washington he had missed her less than he'd expected. As he dressed, she pulled the covers over herself and turned away from him.

On the bedside table was a copy of a novel by Graham Greene, *The Quiet American*. It wasn't the sort of book Cynthia would ever have picked up on her own. It must be something her new lover had left behind, and Borden wondered how he had failed to notice it when he came into the room. He went to the table and picked it up.

"Are you enjoying this?" he said.

"What?" she said. She was still looking away.

"This book. *The Quiet American*."

"I haven't started it yet."

Borden checked the front of the book to see if the man's name was in it. Nothing. He finished dressing.

"So this is the end," he said.

"I guess," she said. She turned back toward him. She was crying.

"You're sure," he said.

She nodded.

He reached out his hand, and she grasped it.

"Goodbye, Borden. I'm sorry."

"Don't be," he said. "What happens happens."

Back in his own apartment he took a shower and, as if deliberately repeating the events of the afternoon, stood naked in the darkness by the window and looked out over the city. He wanted to catch the feeling again, of himself as an observer, the privileged observer of a secret history. He watched the lights of the cars move through the streets. In a dingy room an informer was offering bits of gossip and trying to talk his handler into offering more money. On the downtown streets, a team of watchers was observing a Russian diplomat who had nothing surreptitious on his mind, but was performing various manoeuvres to lose them just for the practice. Borden climbed into his bed.

He picked up a magazine and had read a couple of pages when the phone rang. It must be Cynthia. She was the only one who knew that he was back. He let it ring three times before he climbed from bed to answer it.

"Borden Denny?" A man's voice, with an American accent.

"Yes."

"This is Jack Tamblyn. Bud Hurnick suggested I give you a call. Just to say hello and welcome back."

"You know Bud?"

"Old friends. I'm at the Embassy here, commercial counsellor. Bud told me a lot of good things about you, Borden. They were impressed with you."

"I was impressed too."

"How about a drink one of these days? Bud says he's taught you to drink bourbon."

"Too much of it last night. My head's still aching."

"You know the only cure for that?"

"What?"

"A good lay. Straighten you right out."

"I'll remember that."

Borden could see Cynthia sitting up in bed, the narrow pointed breasts, the look on her face as she told him they were through. Now that it was too late, he felt angry, bitter words come into his mind.

"Why don't you call me next week?" the voice was saying. "We could meet downtown."

"Sure."

"Great, Borden. See you then."

The phone clicked as he hung up, but for a moment Borden stood with the receiver still at his ear, as if he might hear something more, something secret and important, but there was only the soft crackling of static.

Borden was up early in the morning and made his way to a neighbourhood convenience store for a few groceries. After he'd made and eaten breakfast, he set out to walk to his office. He would be there ahead of McAllister. He tried always to be there ahead of McAllister. It gave him a bit of an edge.

Officially, McAllister was still a member of the RCMP, and he was working in the new office as chief liaison with the RCMP Security Service. As soon as the new service was officially in existence, he'd be given a senior appointment. McAllister hated the undefined position in which he found himself, and he wasn't an easy man to begin with. An uncomfortable man to work for, and Borden needed every bit of edge he could get. McAllister respected hard work; no one would work harder than Borden Denny.

The uniformed Mountie at the doorway to their section greeted him as he arrived.

"Nice to see you back," he said.

Borden wondered if it was indiscreet to make any reference to where he'd been. Decided it was.

"You keep everything under control, Sal?"

"Doing my best."

In his office, Borden found the predictable pile of paper, mostly copies of memos of which he was the last and most junior recipient. He read and initialled those that were for return, read and annotated the others, made a few notes on his calendar.

Halfway through the morning, when he had almost finished the pile of memos and was preparing to file them, his phone rang and McAllister's secretary summoned him. Crawford's manner was as always sharply military.

Borden made his way down the hall to McAllister's office. When Borden walked in, McAllister didn't stand to greet him, just looked up from the desk and nodded, the big frame filling the wooden chair. He

always felt a certain hostility from McAllister, who resented Borden's lack of military discipline — not being called sir by the lower orders.

"Sit down," McAllister said.

Borden sat in one of the nondescript chairs. The
office seemed almost deliberately without character,
furniture unmatched and without any distinction of
age or newness. No pictures of wife and family.

"I suppose it's still warm down there," McAllister
said. He made the remark sound like the beginning
of an interrogation.

"It was when I left."

"Was the trip useful?"

As if he didn't think there was much chance it
would be.

"It's quite a place."

"Makes this look like a small-town operation,
doesn't it?"

"It's a big enterprise," Borden said. "Gives you an
idea of the possibilities."

"Now that you're back, what do you have in front
of you?"

"I assume I'll start on more background papers for
the draft legislation."

"How long is that going to take?" McAllister asked
with an ironic inflection.

"It's not up to me."

"I know that, but you've worked on it. I can't get
any sense out of those others."

'Those others' being the senior civilian advisers
who were responsible for steering the new security
service through the difficult political and bureau-
cratic waters.

"I understand they've already had five meetings with the Treasury Board about how much organizational detail the estimates should give, and nothing's settled."

"You're as bad as the rest of them. Can't give a simple answer."

"If they can settle the policy questions, the legislation could be ready in six months."

"Which means two years or more."

"Could be."

"Anything I should know about your trip before you go back to polishing commas?"

"There is one thing that came up."

"What's that?"

"Some information they just got. It has a connection here."

"Are they sending it through to the Security Service?" McAllister said, and suddenly Borden didn't know just how to answer. It had seemed simple before.

"Well, it seems like a small thing. At first."

"And your friends down there think we won't pursue it."

"They didn't think it would have a high priority."

McAllister was watching him. Borden was aware of what an effective interrogator the man would be.

"I suppose they suggested you could look into it on your own," McAllister said, and his eyes moved away and waited.

"If I had time."

"And who would get the reports on this private investigation?" The voice was soft and very cold.

"I expect you would."

"Is that what they suggested?"

"It wasn't discussed." In fact, Borden had been aware that they had very deliberately not brought up that point.

"And their man here in Ottawa? Has he happened to contact you since you got back?"

"He called last night. Just to say hello."

McAllister was watching him again. Borden knew he'd made a wrong step. He shouldn't have told McAllister at all.

"They asked you to investigate this on your own, but they didn't make any suggestions about who you'd report to, and their man in Ottawa just happened to phone after you got back. The day you got back."

"Are you accusing me of something?"

McAllister stopped for a moment, and picked up a pencil. He made a note on a pad in front of him.

"You have to admire their persistence," he said.

Borden didn't answer. Less said the better now.

"So what is this matter that came up?" McAllister said.

"Some reports from Greece. They were able to identify a Russian agent. He'd been there for some time and hadn't been spotted. Then he had a serious illness. I guess he got careless."

"And I suppose his brother-in-law is running a restaurant right here in Ottawa."

"They ran the name through the computer."

"And what is the name?"

"Petroff. Nikos Petroff."

"And when the computer heard Petroff," McAllister snapped, "it brought up the Gouzenko case from

1945. And the Canadians like Fred Rose and Sam Carr who were identified as spies in Gouzenko's documents."

McAllister knew. Borden was shaken. Was this some kind of game the Americans were playing with him? His shock must have showed. McAllister was looking at him and nodding.

"When we reinvestigated the Gouzenko file in the sixties, I was one of the men who did it."

"Petroff was never caught, was he?"

"He knew we were coming, and he didn't wait around."

"Did you know he'd turned up in Greece?"

McAllister didn't answer directly.

"Have they notified the Greek authorities?" he said.

"It was too late," Borden said.

"Vanished again?"

"He died."

"So they want you to chase a dead man?"

"Since he was still active, they thought he might have connections here."

McAllister stood up, walked to the window, then without even looking out, walked back to the desk, stood for a second, then walked to the window again. The gestures all seemed a little rigid, automatic. He was very angry.

"It's the perfect case, isn't it?" he said. "Set you to studying ancient history. Perfectly innocent. An investigation that everybody knows about. You can talk it over with their men here without feeling compromised, but you're working for them. They've got hold of a man who's in on the planning of the new agency. A *little* secret to start with."

"I've told you about it. They never suggested it should be a secret. That's not what they wanted."

"What they want is for you to feel you have a special relationship with them. Look back at old cases to see if we made mistakes. Starting asking yourself how Communists like Petroff and Freda Linton and Sam Carr managed to disappear before we could arrest them."

"There is some new information. If Petroff was still active in Greece, some of his old connections might still be active here."

"I went back over the ground fifteen years ago, Mr Denny. We double-checked all the information. Gouzenko is dead and so is that case. What they're telling you is to look back and check work I've done."

"I don't think of it that way."

"Well, that's what it amounts to. And if I want some smart-ass young lawyer to check my old cases, I'll ask."

He turned back from the window and stared at Borden. His face was pale and still.

"You stick to the fine points of the law, and leave investigation to those who know what they're doing."

Borden left without answering.

4

What McAllister would have liked was to cuff young Denny across the side of the head and knock him out of his chair. It was what he deserved, but no one would ever do it. McAllister looked around his office. It soured his mouth. It made him want to spit.

In principle, his position here was an important one, and he was probably meant for something good when the new security service was finally established, but it all went so slowly that by the time the job was ready he'd be forced to retire. He couldn't imagine what he might do then. He had no hobbies, no family. He disliked gardening, woodwork, all the things that men were supposed to have to fill their empty hours.

Compulsory retirement was still some way off, but it was there, in the distance, like a storm on the prairie, so far away on the horizon that you could study its progress as you waited for it to arrive. The prairie was like a rattlesnake, they said, it always gave

warning before it struck. Maybe he should go back
and finish out his time there. He remembered what it
was like to be deep in a prairie coulee, to climb the
steep hills toward the sky, as if to reach a height of
land, but instead to come to the endless flat earth.
You could go down, into a valley, a river course, but
never up. There was only earth and sky.

Here in Ottawa, he lived among shades and shad-
ows. For now, his friends in the RCMP went on with
the real work, while he wandered in this fog of plans
and promises. He attended meetings, like the one
yesterday on the question of agents among the recent
Polish immigrants, but he had no active role. He
passed on messages. He consulted. Dreadful word.
He tried to hold together two worlds that had nothing in common. The men in the RCMP Security Service distrusted him because he was an outsider now, a
civil servant working for the Solicitor-General's
office. The civil servants distrusted or ignored him
because he was only a policeman with no education
beyond high school and the practical learning of the
years in the western detachments.

He tried to remember why he'd applied for the Security Service and couldn't quite. In the small towns
of Saskatchewan, he'd always been something of an
odd man out. He didn't have the easygoing ways that
made a policeman popular and effective, half his
work done automatically by the trust he won among
the people around him. He was too private for that.
But once he had joined the Security Service he'd
known he was home. His solitude and silence. His
penchant for second thoughts and third and fourth;
his passion for knowing, for seeing clearly; they all

fitted. His persistence was endless. One after another, he ran down the Russians who misbehaved. He came to have a reputation among them for the dogged pursuit. The Security Service joked that the Russians stopped everything the moment he stepped out of the door of the building.

One of the Russians, a KGB man working under diplomatic cover, had gone so far as to send McAllister a present on the eve of his expulsion from Canada. It had been delivered to McAllister by mail, with a small card attached. *You need a good Russian wife.* Those words were typed inside the card. The gift was one of those bright peasant dolls of turned wood which opened to reveal another doll, which also opened to reveal another.

McAllister had taken it to the technical people and had it examined for any sort of radio implant, but they declared it innocent and returned it to him. It was no more than it appeared to be, a Russian toy. It sat in the living room of his house, and the round eyes stared at him as he dawdled over his evening drink.

His reputation as a solitary had reached even the Russians, it seemed. Well, they were right, he was a better spycatcher for having no distractions, no other loyalties.

Did they know that now he was effectively, if not officially, on the shelf? When they set out to suborn civil servants and research scientists, were they aware that it wouldn't be McAllister who kept a watch on them? It wouldn't take much for one of their journalists to learn it, and quite legally too. McAllister hated to think that they could know his teeth had been pulled. A toothless old bear with the promise of a new set of teeth. Sometime. Later. When the clever boys got the new thing all painted and polished.

Clever boys like Borden Denny. The Americans had a nerve setting Denny off on an investigation. They were like the Russians that way; they'd try anything and they trusted no one. Clever boys tying themselves in knots. They didn't realize how simple it all was. That was always his secret in dealing with the Russians. To remember that the more complicated they try to make it the simpler it will be to spot. A man with something to hide behaves differently from a man with nothing to hide. If you came to it from police work, you had learned early on that most criminals give themselves away sooner or later. There was something artificial about concealment that led to its destruction.

He would have to keep an eye on Denny. He was in one hell of a hurry. Education made men ambitious and impatient. When McAllister joined the RCMP, it was a job, and he only expected to do his job and take his pay. Education gave young men the impression that they were important people and that some sort of significant destiny was waiting for them just around the corner.

McAllister wondered if he should bring the Russian doll into the office. There was something about the lifeless painted eyes that was good for him. He liked to feel the bitter irony of the Russian who'd sent it to him. The anger was his reward for work well done. The doll was his wife, in a way, the perpetual observer of his life. Now and then, he thought how it might have been if he had married, if he'd got over the break with Jean, the sense of betrayal when she abandoned him for Malcolm Fraser suddenly, without warning. He had always thought that he and Jean would get married. But the wide wooden eyes of the doll stared him out of countenance and revealed that thought for what it was, a sentimental dream. The wooden doll was his wife.

He wondered if Denny had a woman; he wasn't married. A few years back, a man involved in an illicit relationship would have been thought a security risk, but it was accepted now. The next thing, they'd be asking him to take on queers. Not, he hoped, in his day. It might be all right to have perverts in some parts of the civil service, but not here. There was too much at stake.

Had anyone ever thought that of him? He had, after all, never married. But it must be clear from the way a man walked and talked that he wasn't one of them.

He thought of young Denny going out of the place at night and into some woman's bed. McAllister felt a kind of anger that might have been envy, but he put it down. He'd made his choices. But trying to deal with the politicians and clever boys enraged him sometimes. Denny assuming that he could start an investigation without telling anyone.

He'd have lunch with one of his friends from RCMP headquarters. He needed to feel part of the real world again.

McAllister went out into the hall where his secretary, Crawford, was typing.

"What do you think, Crawford? Are they going to tell us we have to start hiring queers?"

Crawford looked up at him, startled.

"No, sir," he said. "I don't think so."

At lunch McAllister sat across the table from Cliff Slater, who had been a protégé of his a few years before. Cliff always had a flat, meaty face, and now he'd put on weight his features seemed more than ever opaque and resistant to any outward impression.

The young Italian waitress took their order and walked away from the table. Cliff studying her retreating haunches. His face never changed expression, but his eyes followed her until she was out of sight.

"So what's been happening?" McAllister said.

"Don't they tell you?"

Was Cliff being careful with him?

"Officially they tell me everything, but now that I'm not in the same office as the rest of you, I can't really keep up."

"But you're upstairs. With the big boys."

"The big boys don't know ass from elbow. By the time they figure it out, I'll be so out of date I'll be useless to them or anybody else."

"Everybody says you've been promoted. That you're on your way to the stars."

"Who says that?"

"Réal for one."

"Choquette?"

"Yes."

"I think he wanted the job. I don't know why."

"Why did you take it?"

"Plain damn foolishness. I didn't think about it long enough to realize the whole thing takes forever. Lawyers and politicians and guys from the Harvard

Business School. Takes them three days to move a comma."

"Why don't you quit?"

"I can't now. It would look like a failure."

The girl came back with bowls of soup. Cliff stared at her breasts.

"So tell me," McAllister said when the girl had gone away, "what's going on in the real world."

"Real? Funny, I always figure real is choking hell out of some junkie who's trying to swallow twenty caps of heroin. This stuff is Disneyland. Going to the movies."

"Are they changing people at the Embassy?"

"Yeah, some of them. We haven't quite figured it out yet."

"I'd guess it will be a double switch. First the new bosses will want to get a few people out, but they won't put the new ones in right away. They'll run through a few dummies. Either that or they'll send in one regiment to set up the technical resources and a new one to exploit them."

"Why do you think that?"

"With Andropov on top, it's the first time that a KGB man has been in power. That means two things. The KGB has power, but also the KGB has no secrets. The man at the top knows all the little ways they cook the books. So, for a while at least, they're going to have to be very careful. No big mistakes. Andropov knows their names and their jobs and they can't blame someone else for their mistakes. But he's going to demand changes and improvements to show how smart he is. So it's all going to be very disciplined and professional. Look for the cool ones. Or they might bring back a few old-timers. People they think we've forgotten."

Cliff was watching him, the heavy face expressionless and yet attentive.

"They shouldn't have moved you out."

"And I shouldn't have gone, but I did, and it's too damned late now. All I can do is try to get this new business functioning and maybe I can go back to work."

"You hear the Cuban desk is expanding?"

"I heard they're looking for guys who can talk Spanish."

"The Americans are screaming for action all the time. They claim the Nicaraguans are running wild up here."

"Are they?"

"I don't think we know."

"I suppose the French guys learn Spanish faster. It's almost the same language, isn't it?"

"But they talk it with an accent just like us. Where are we going to recruit guys who speak Spanish?"

"What about Italians?"

"Yeah, they all look the same to me too, but they aren't even close. The Americans have thousands of them. Mexicans and Cubans and Puerto Ricans from a generation or so back. Good loyal citizens who can talk perfect Spanish. They can't wait to send us one or two."

"They're pushing you too, are they?"

"You having trouble with them?"

"Hints. I think they'd like to get in on the ground floor. Like putting their microphones right in the steel frame of the buildings."

The waitress claimed their bowls. Cliff stared.

"You keep staring at that waitress."

"Looks good enough to eat, doesn't she?"

"It wouldn't take the Russians long to figure out your weakness."

"I just look. I don't touch."

At the end of the meal the two men shook hands and separated. McAllister drove downtown and out Sussex Drive past the prime minister's house and the governor general's where Mounties in red tunics stood guard. As if he were following a secret voice, he went on to drive past the Russian Embassy. No one visible as he went by; but his blood stirred at the sight. He wondered if the watchers had noticed him slow down just a little, if his licence number would go down in their reports. He looked at the speedometer. He hadn't slowed enough that any watcher would think it significant. He was tempted to go back again, make a second pass or a third, to play a game with them. Even to stop across the road. He had thought that lunch with Cliff Slater would help, but he was even more frustrated now, more aware that he was out of the game, lost on some foolish futile errand. Irritable and impatient, he decided not to return to the office for the afternoon. It was years since he'd done such a thing; he drove himself home instead. He went into the living-room. As impersonal as a hotel room. Except for the bottle of rum. The doll. He took the Russian doll from its place on a side table and turned the two pieces to open it. Inside was another, smaller but identical doll, with the same wide eyes. He opened it. Inside was another. He opened that. Finally he came on the last, solid doll, which

stared at him with a smaller version of the same wide
eyes. The wooden pieces lay on the table. He reas-
sembled them.

It all seemed, in some way he couldn't explain, significant.

5

Sunlight was a rarity at this season, something to be treasured. He stood on the church lawn where he'd been picking up the twigs and branches that had been dropped here by last night's high wind. He looked toward the sun, which, having passed the zenith, seemed immediately to suggest sunset and darkness. The days were only a momentary interruption of one long dark winter night.

He heard the distant report of a rifle. Deer hunters. He had seen cars parked by the road this morning as he made his way to the church.

In the strong wind, a falling branch had swung sideways as it came away and had cracked one of Margaret's storm windows. He had promised to fix it for her after he finished at the church.

He put the twigs and branches in a small pile beside the box that held the garbage cans. He would tie them in a bundle when he put them out for collection. Then he crossed the road toward the high frame house where Margaret lived. It needed a coat of paint, and it had a look of emptiness, as if most of the rooms were unlived in. Blinds were pulled and faded or windows without blinds and curtains stared like hollow eyes.

As he was crossing the road, he felt once again, as he had so often recently, that he was being watched. He stopped, turned back to the church, let himself in, went through the building and out a back door so that he reappeared at a far corner. There was no sign of anyone. He wondered again if his mind was going. It was a terrifying prospect.

Once again he crossed the road to Margaret's house. She was waiting for him at the door.

"Malcolm," she said, "who are you playing hide-and-seek with?"

"No one."

"That seems unlikely."

He didn't answer.

"I made coffee," she said.

They were standing in a long dark hallway at the end of which was a bright kitchen. She led the way toward it. The house was cold and she was wearing three sweaters, a thin red one, that showed at the wrists and neck, a heavier brown one and a mauve cardigan. Below the cuffs of her jeans, she displayed pale-blue socks. She walked down the hall in a pair of fluffy slippers.

"It frightened me half to death," she said over her shoulder.

"What?"

"That window shattering like that. I thought they'd come for me."

"Who?"

"I wasn't quite sure. Maybe the same people you were playing hide-and-seek with."

The kitchen was small and crowded. In one corner was a pile of magazines, in another, garden tools and a cardboard box full of potatoes. A wet mop stood in a pail of grey water in the middle of the floor. He looked for a chair and had to move an old coat to sit on it.

"Is your leg bad today, Malcolm?" she said. "You seem to be favouring it."

"Aching a bit. The limp gets more noticeable every year, doesn't it? There was a time when scarcely anyone could tell."

"The war, wasn't it?"

He nodded.

"Where were you when you were wounded?"

She was lifting a coffee percolator off the stove, which was crowded with unwashed dishes.

"Greece."

She put the percolator down on the table and turned toward him, her heavy eyelids sinking over her eyes as her features made a large gesture of puzzlement.

"There was no Canadian units in Greece."

"You sound pretty sure of that."

"My father served in the First War. In the Second, he followed the movements of the Canadian forces quite minutely. It was the main topic of conversation over breakfast."

"Odd for a clergyman."

"I always suspected that he knew more about the fighting spirit than he did about the Holy Spirit. What were you doing in Greece?"

"Working behind enemy lines."

"A secret agent." She poured the coffee into a cracked cup and surveyed him. "Yes," she said, "I can see that."

She poured herself a cup.

"And now you're a sexton."

"Janitor is my word for it."

"The Church of England has its own style."

"I've noticed."

"You never came to church with your wife."

"No."

In silence they drank the coffee.

"It's kind of you to offer to do the window," Margaret said. "That Naylor boy who puts them up for me is husky, but I don't think he has much upstairs. I'd hate to trust him with a job requiring any skill."

"Doesn't take much skill to change a piece of glass."

"Not for you, Malcolm, but you're clever with your hands."

"Do you have a ladder?"

"You'll find it in the shed."

As he climbed the ladder toward the broken window, he could smell a sharp edge to the November wind. It smelled like snow. Taking down the window, he could see into Margaret's bedroom. The covers were pulled up but not tucked in, and on top of them lay a snow-shovel. He wondered if Margaret had it there for protection. He laid the window on a piece of wood and used his heel to break away most of the remaining glass, then pulled out the last pieces by hand and scraped away the old putty with a rusty knife he'd found in Margaret's shed.

He drove downtown to get glass and putty, and

while he was on the main street he stopped in at the
Post Office to pick up his mail. He hadn't bothered
for the last few days. He got little mail except for
bills.

There was a letter from Vancouver, but it wasn't
Edward's handwriting.

Dear Mr Fraser,

I don't know if you might have heard from Edward. I guess that's why I'm writing you and to tell
you if you don't know. He walked out on us a few
weeks ago. I don't know where he is. I got a job and
I'm managing so far but I don't know where to turn.
With two kids, everything costs so much. We had our
problems, but doesn't everybody? Most men don't
just leave and not get in touch. I'm not asking for
anything, but you did always seem interested in the
kids, the times we saw you. I guess things must be
hard for you too after what happened to Edward's
mother. I thought maybe all that had something to
do with him going away. He never really seemed the
same after he came back from the funeral.

Frank just joined the Cubs. I told him his Dad was
away on a trip for a while. If you hear from Edward,
maybe you could let me know.

Yours sincerely,

Connie

He read the letter twice. Then he folded it,

returned it to the envelope and threw it down on the
seat beside him.

He had never known Edward, he decided. Somewhere they had missed each other, and when he tried
to imagine the situation, how Edward had simply
packed up and walked out, there was nothing. No
hint of understanding. He needed Jean to explain it
to him. She had understood the boy's mysterious
coolness or at least had offered explanations that
seemed to make some sense.

Could she have foreseen this? Perhaps it did have
some connection with her death.

He must do something to help Connie. Send
money. There wasn't much to send. Perhaps he
should sell the house and send her the proceeds. He
must send some sort of present or letter to young
Frank. He could go out there for Christmas. Unless
Edward had come back by then.

Suddenly he knew that Edward wouldn't be back
by Christmas. That he would never be back. But how
did he know that without Jean to work it out, to tell
him?

Edward would never be back. He must take over
what responsibility he could for the children. He
would send a hundred dollars; probably he could
manage that. If he didn't act now, he would lose
touch. Connie would forget about him, and when she
found some new man, the children would never hear
of him again. Maybe he'd suggest that Frank come
and spend the summer with him. It wasn't a bad
place for a boy; there was fishing and swimming, perhaps canoeing.

What made him think that he would be any help to his grandchildren when he had failed with Edward?

The first thing was to write to her and send what money he could.

He drove back to Margaret's house, and as he worked on the window, moving it round to the front of the house to be in the sun which warmed him a bit and perhaps helped a little to keep the putty soft while he worked with it, he thought angrily of his son, the bland face that had never told him anything. There was something unmanly about the boy, always had been; something self-excusing. They should have had more children; Edward had been able to take everything for granted. He had slid easily through life, never forced to confront danger or disaster. Perhaps every father resented his son's apparent freedom. He remembered his own father's resentment when he said he was leaving the farm to join the RCMP. He might as well have said he was running away to join the circus.

He saw both faces in his mind, his father's and his son's, and for the first time in his life, he realized that they looked a lot alike. And he had been equally cut off from both of them. He saw Margaret watching him from inside one of the windows, and he waved. Perhaps he would mention the letter to her. No. He would keep it to himself. As he always had. Except with Jean. God, how he missed her.

Margaret stood by the window of the front bedroom, the room that had been her father's when he was alive, to watch the man working on the lawn below, the angled light of the November afternoon painting his body with patches of gold. She reached into the pocket of her cardigan and took out her glasses. She put them on, and now the figure was revealed in sharp detail, his hands moving quickly along the edge of the glass as he slid the putty into place and trimmed it with a knife.

The grass around his feet was long and a deep green, and the wind had blown the leaves into a curve along the line of bushes at the edge; a few lay singly where Malcolm worked, as if they had been dropped there carefully as decoration or to communicate some obscure message. They seemed important in the dark sunlight, as if they must have some significance. Leaf. Leaf. Leaf.

To the left across the road, Margaret saw the aged red brick of the church building. She might almost have been a child again expecting to see the small quick figure of her father appear from the church door and pace rapidly to the house. And if she had seen him coming Margaret would have hurried down the stairs to meet him, to find out if he had calls to make at the homes of parishioners or at the hospital and to plan what time they might eat dinner. And he would go up to her mother's room, Margaret would hear a few quiet words spoken, and then he would be gone and Margaret would go up and ask her mother if she wanted a cup of tea or perhaps a slice of toast. The woman would be staring at a point on the wallpaper where there was a small rip. Sometimes it seemed to Margaret that her mother had caused the paper to tear with the pure force of her gaze. She never turned those eyes on Margaret, and Margaret was grateful, for she always felt that if she met her mother's eyes there would be some dangerous revelation. In church when she came to the place in the Communion service where the words were spoken *especially those for whom our prayers are desired*, Margaret tried to think of her mother, but she never felt sure that her mother did desire prayer. Sometimes Margaret felt that the secret of her illness was that she didn't believe in God or the church.

There was some terrible secret in the house; Margaret had felt that from the time she was a child, but even now, as an old woman, she didn't know just what the secret was. Her mother was ill and unhappy. Her father had lived without most of the comforts that marriage was supposed to provide until Margaret was old enough to cook and keep the house and organize his life. There was, she always supposed, no physical contact between her parents. They had slept in different rooms for as long as Margaret could remember, though presumably they had been together to conceive her. A life without wasn't such a disaster, was it? Margaret had lived without. Perhaps it was worse for a man.

It was not the sort of thing her father could ever have told her. As if he told her anything. He was polite and silent. Even when he grew old he kept conversation rigorously superficial. He must, presumably, discuss God and his works with the parishioners. He went to comfort them on their death-beds. Perhaps it was like his sermons. The words were there, and they made sense, and yet behind them, there was nothing but more words. They were made out of books. Words were a defence of his final

terrible privacy. There was always the liturgy, a
prayer for every occasion.

Malcolm turned the window on its side and began
to run putty down another edge of the glass. When
she looked at Malcolm, she knew that someone was
there. Not like her father. Malcolm was solid. In his
own way, a private man, but the privacy didn't seem
like a way of hiding. When he looked at you, you
knew that he saw you. When her father had looked at
her, she often felt as if he saw no one there at all. She
became invisible in his gaze. Malcolm seemed to see
everything, to be aware of its weight and texture and
colour. He lived on earth.

Had that always been with him? she wondered.
Perhaps he had learned it in the war. *Working behind
enemy lines.* You could see that on his face, as if his
whole life had been lived like that. Like his cleaning
the church. It was done carefully, conscientiously,
and in silence. He came in when no one was there
(except Margaret, and she was accepted by everyone
as part of the furniture) and did his work and left.
And then in the evenings and on Sundays, the rector
and the congregation gathered and did all those
things that were set to be done, and Malcolm's presence was there while he was absent. He was at his
house at the edge of the bush.

She wasn't surprised that he had never attended
church. He didn't need it. He was at home on the
earth and in his own skin. His clothes, the green work
pants, old hand-knitted sweater, worn windbreaker,
were nondescript and yet there was a propriety, an
almost military sense of function and fitness to them.
He was a man who would age and die without decay.

Why had he been playing games when he came across here, going in one door of the church and out the other? She remembered the car she had seen outside the church a few mornings ago, the man who watched her go in. He wasn't someone from around here. It was the wrong kind of face. She had lived here in Eastern Ontario for so many years that she could recognize strangers by their features and dress. The man she'd seen in the car was from some other place.

Did Malcolm have secrets? If so they wouldn't be like her father's, unspeakable and perhaps incomprehensible. They would be deliberate and purposeful.

He had finished the window and placed it against the tree and was walking toward the house. She observed, as she often had, how firmly he walked, with only the slight rhythmic intervention of the damaged leg. She would like him to tell her how it had happened. Perhaps some day he would. She went down to meet him at the door of the house.

"You have some newspaper?" he said. "I'll wash that window before I put it back up."

"I don't read newspapers, not usually. I have a few magazines."

"The paper in magazines isn't right," he said. "Do you have paper towels or a cloth?"

Margaret went to the kitchen and tried to find something suitable. She opened the drawer where she kept things for which she could find no other place. Halfway open, it was jammed by a large piece of wood that she'd put in for a reason that she could no longer remember. She felt angry and embarrassed that she lived in such a state of chaos.

Malcolm stood patiently at the end of the hall while
she took out a jar of rusty nails, more pieces of wood,
a torn sweater, a tin of cat food left from the days
when she had Popper, and a large piece of rock.
Nothing useful. Leaving everything on the floor
where she'd dropped it, she gave him a tea-towel.

"Vinegar?" he said.

"What?"

"It helps take off the grease from the putty."

"Over here."

As she reached toward the food cupboard, she
tripped over the jar of nails and spilled it. Malcolm
moved as if to pick them up.

"No," she said. "Don't bother. They should be
thrown out anyway."

As she opened the food cupboard, she realized that
it needed cleaning, but she seized the vinegar and
quickly closed the door. Malcolm was at the sink
pouring water on the tea-towel. She gave him the vinegar, and he made his way back out, and Margaret
began to pick up the nails and put the pieces of wood
back in the drawer. She looked at the jar of nails,
many of them bent, most of them rusted, and knew
that she should throw it out, but instead she laid it
back where she had found it. She was afraid to throw
it out. Like taking just a small spoonful out of a house
of sand. Even that might be enough to undermine
the whole structure. Things in Margaret's house lay
where they fell because it was too dangerous to move
them. If she put things in order, she would be able to
see clearly, and that was altogether too frightening a
prospect. Let things lie. Don't think of alternatives.
Nothing could be any different than it is.

When her father told her she was needed at home and couldn't attend teacher's college, nothing more could have been said. When her mother died, and she hoped they might move to Kingston or Ottawa, the move could not have been made. When Ernie McKay offered her a full-time job clerking in the store, there was no other choice but to stay with her father who was old and ill.

Nothing could be any different than it is.

If she were to get rid of the jar of nails, then she might dispose of the pieces of wood, the tin of cat food, the curtain rod, the three ancient mason jars, and if she did that then she might throw out the albums of photographs, the notes for her father's sermons, her mother's old hats, and if once she began she would end by setting the house on fire and tearing off her clothes and dancing naked on the lawn of the church as she watched it burn.

Nothing could be any different than it is.

She heard Malcolm moving the ladder, and she went up the stairs to the bedroom, to watch him. There was no harm in that. She stood just inside the door of the room where each night she lay alone and prayed for sleep to come. There was a snow-shovel on her bed, and she couldn't remember why it was there. Not to remember such a thing. She must be insane. A dotty old maid. Outside the window, she saw Malcolm's figure against the sky, as he balanced on the wooden rungs of the ladder and set the heavy window in its place. He saw her watching him, and his eyes were level and calm. Behind him, the air was filling with clouds, and the light grew thinner and harder. Light was rare and precious on these

November days. She looked at the man's solid body, out there in the real world, and felt that she was a ghost watching him. She would have liked to reach through the glass and touch him, to prove to herself that she was real, to draw him in with her. She glanced toward the bed.

She didn't really know what men and women did there, except in a general way, of course, from dogs and childhood stories and columns of advice in the magazines. But she didn't *know*. If it was comfort or ecstasy or both at once. How that could be.

A boy had kissed her once, on her eighteenth birthday. It had been unremarkable. But sometimes in dreams she knew what it must be like.

Perhaps Malcolm would fall from the ladder, and she would go to him, and she would have to touch him to lift him from the ground. She could bring him in the house and look after him.

She stopped herself. Nothing could change. There was only God to pray to who made it right that everything was as it was. She wasn't starving or freezing to death.

She was. Frozen. Starved. Malcolm had turned the catches to hold the window in place, and now he was going down the ladder, first his torso and then his shoulders and then his head disappearing, and there was only the grey sky. She heard the ladder bump against the house as he took it down, and she could feel the soft bumping come through the floor and up through her feet. He was finished. He would go. The sky would grow dark and darker, and in the night she would be alone.

Once more she went down the stairs, and as Malcolm came back from putting the ladder away she met him by the front door. The wind was colder now, and she pulled the cardigan across her chest against the chill. She thanked him, and his face was level and calm. He was a good man; that he could exist in the world was evidence enough of God's mercy. She mustn't be ungrateful. Perhaps she would empty out her mother's old room and her father's and try to rent them. It would be good for her to have strangers in the house, and the money would make things easier.

She watched Malcolm as he went to his car. His presence gave her confidence and hope.

6

The meeting had gone well. Borden had presented a report based on his discussion of the legislative setup in Washington. It had been short and to the point, and no one had been able to offer any criticism of it, and the planning for the next meeting would be based on the way he'd organized the material. Now as he made his way down the hall, he saw Beaudry from Justice waiting for him.

"Good piece of work," he said, as Borden came up to him. "Should have more goddam lawyers in here. They know how to think." Beaudry's English was fluent, not heavily accented, but his 'goddams' were just a bit too colloquial. The civil servant as tough guy.

"Don't say that to McAllister."

"McAllister's just an old cop. He'll do what he's told."

They made their way down the stairs.

"You want to go have a drink?" Beaudry said.

"I already arranged to meet someone."

"*Plus jolie que moi*, eh?"

"Don't I wish."

Borden regretted not being able to have the drink with Beaudry. He was one of the heavyweights at Justice, and it would be useful to have a contact at the senior ministry. But he had the appointment with Jack Tamblyn. That could be useful too. He parted from Beaudry at the door and made his way through the dark streets to the bar where he'd suggested they meet. Tamblyn's advice on how to recognize him was simple; look for an old-fashioned moustache. When Borden walked into the bar, he looked around and saw him. He was right. There was a hint of Clark Gable or Ronald Colman in the face. They shook hands over the table, and Borden sat down as Tamblyn waved for the waiter. They were in a corner some distance from the piano bar.

The waiter was standing beside them.

"Rye and water," Borden said.

"And I'll have another."

The waiter moved away.

"I always drink rye when I'm in Ottawa," Tamblyn said. "When in Rome."

"I guess that's why I drank bourbon in Washington."

"Glad to be back in Canada?"

"In some ways."

"I was in Washington yesterday. Saw Bud Hurnick and Bernie Fedor. They were asking about you."

Tamblyn glanced out the window to the Mall where a young man and woman were walking by hand in hand. Borden thought of Cynthia. He kept expecting to see her with a man, but he never had.

Once or twice he had thought of phoning her, but he had stopped himself.

"Bud says that you two are up to something together."

Tamblyn was watching him. Friendly, smiling.

"In a way," Borden said.

The waiter was moving toward them.

"You're not married, are you, Borden?" Tamblyn said, irrelevantly.

"No."

The waiter put down the drinks and Tamblyn nodded to him.

"I like to have a drink after work," he said. "Relax a bit before I go home to play Daddy."

"How many kids do you have?"

"Two. They really love it here. They like the French in school, you know? When they see their friends in Washington, they get to show off."

Borden lifted his glass.

"Cheers," he said.

"Cheers." He drank. "Bud was interested in how things were going on this project you guys got."

"He tell you about it?"

"Not really. The sacred 'need to know' principle, I guess."

Borden watched him, the way his eyes moved. He didn't think he was telling the truth.

"Bud asked me to tell you that he was waiting to hear."

"He'll hear. If anything develops."

Tamblyn picked up his glass and took a large swallow of straight rye. His head was nodding agreeably, as if they had just concluded some important arrangement.

"Bud asked me to offer my help, Borden. If it was of any use to you."

To slow his response, Borden reached for his own drink. They were walking close to the border, and he didn't want to go over it by accident. He was still overexcited from the success of the meeting this afternoon. When he drank, the rye seemed to have no taste.

"Like what?" he said.

"Well, we have resources. It would depend on what you needed."

Borden couldn't quite believe that the offer was being made. Back off, fast, some inner voice told him.

"I'll keep it in mind," he said.

"I understand you're working on pretty tight budgets these days."

"Isn't everyone?"

"If you had expenses . . . needed to put out some cash here and there . . ." he was pausing between phrases, as if measuring his words, as if leaving time for them to sink in, "we might be able to help."

There was something intimate and condescending in his manner.

"You're offering me money?" Borden said, abruptly, to wake the American up to the fact that Borden knew the implications of the conversation.

"For expenses."

"Don't you think that could get me in trouble? Taking money from you?"

"There's always a way to handle these things. And

from my experience, what superior officers care most about is results."

"I'm not so sure about that."

"Shall we order another before we go?" Tamblyn said. Business was over now; they were marking time until they could leave.

"I don't think so."

"Why not?" Tamblyn said winningly. "I'm paying."

"I can pay for my own drink," Borden said.

"Let me. I was the one who suggested the meeting."

"All right."

Borden drained his glass.

"I'd better get on my way," he said.

"Someone waiting?" Tamblyn said.

"Could be."

"Give her my love."

Borden made his way out of the bar. He could feel that Tamblyn was watching, and even when he was outside he had the feeling that there were eyes on him. Would Tamblyn be having him followed? Or McAllister? No. That made no sense. He was just another civil servant worrying about the next step in his career, not part of a secret world, not yet. Not until tomorrow morning when he walked into his office and didn't tell McAllister about Tamblyn's offer. And he wouldn't tell him, he knew. He wouldn't tell anyone. Even if he didn't accept the offer, it might be useful to him. He had heard them make an offer that was more than indiscreet. To offer money to a government servant. To offer to collaborate with him on an unofficial investigation. It was a surprise to him that they would go so far and so fast; they didn't care

how improper the offer was. They did what they
wanted. He had to admire them for that. It was a
contrast to the constant pussyfooting that he was accustomed to, the long discussions and careful eva-
sions. The Americans went for what they wanted.
Perhaps it was the best style for a world in which the
Bulgarians would send a gunman off to kill an incon-
venient pope.

The more he thought about it, the more he ad-
mired Bud Hurnick for the speed and directness of
the approach. If he reported it and there was trouble,
they'd simply say he had misunderstood. It was a mistake to have mentioned the possible investigation to
McAllister in the first place. He should have kept it to
himself.

When he reached his apartment, he opened a tin
of corned beef and sliced it up. From his desk, he
took the notes on Nikos Petroff that he had brought
back from Washington. He put them on the table in
front of him, and as he ate the corned beef between
slices of bread and drank a bottle of beer, he began to
work out how he could start tracing Petroff. He'd
have to find some way to get into the Security Service
files. He wondered if Beaudry might be some help
with that. He could demand to see the files of cases
where the Security Service had got itself in legal
problems, the *Agence Presse Libre* break-in, for example, to see how the decision had been made, and at
what point there should have been a legislative provi-
sion or a clear legislative block. That might work. He
should be having those discussions with the lawyers at
Justice anyway. Once he was in the files, he'd try to
get a look at Petroff's. If he could find a halfway de-

cent excuse, they wouldn't start phoning McAllister to ask questions. Use the Kellock-Taschereau Royal Commission as a precedent or at least argue that it was. Then he could study the whole Gouzenko file.

He made a series of notes, a kind of memo to himself for the outlines of his investigation. If the first steps left him with nothing, he'd let it drop. Maybe McAllister was right, and it had been carefully enough reinvestigated. McAllister was rigid and stuffy, but he wasn't a fool.

Could the Americans already know? Did they know where they were sending him and what he'd find? If that was so, then all they wanted was to get a piece of him. Walk carefully, there were traps all around.

A new copy of *Soviet Affairs* had come, but he couldn't concentrate on it, and he went out for a long walk by the canal to try and tire himself enough for sleep. He stared at the lights reflected in the dark water. The night wind seemed to penetrate his clothes and reach the skin beneath.

He walked for a long time, but when he got back to his apartment he couldn't sleep. He lay in the darkness and waited for morning.

7

They sat across from each other, unmoving, formal, like children at a birthday party waiting to be told when to sing, when to dance, when to eat, in a strange house with strange parents in control. Malcolm looked at the face, as old as his own, the bent hands; arthritic. The face was worn, pale, tired-looking.

"I didn't suppose I'd ever see you again," he said.

"No. It wasn't to be expected."

"I sent you away. All of you."

"Yes."

"But here you are."

"Yes."

Silence. He was waiting for Malcolm to do the talking. He was to be in control, now and always. Malcolm settled back in his chair and let the silence hang in the air. He could hear the soft sound of the wind in the stove-pipes, the sound of the fire in the stove. They waited. The world ended. They waited. Finally the other man spoke.

71

"Your wife is dead."

"Yes."

"Unfortunate."

"That's not an adequate response."

The man folded his hands in front of him. There was something pious about the gesture, something priestly and complacent. It angered Malcolm. Was it meant to? Was his anger deliberately roused to give them a grip on him? If he started to think like that, the man was already winning. Jean was gone; nothing else mattered.

"Your son."

Malcolm didn't answer. The man was a crude physician, poking and prodding, hoping to make the patient flinch in agony, to prove his own power and the patient's need for him.

"He has behaved badly."

"You've been reading my mail. You've been in this house."

The man bowed his head, priestly again. Malcolm was aware of another soft sound in the room. It was the other man's breathing, a little laboured, a little stertorous. He was old and in poor health. Why had they sent him here?

" 'Gentlemen don't read each other's mail,' " Malcolm quoted. "We've come a long way since Stimson said that, haven't we? Secretary of War, he was called. He'd be Secretary of Defence now. We've learned hypocrisy."

"It's good that you can see through American hypocrisy."

"I would have thought you knew better than that,

Peter. To try an ideological approach. You know better."

"I made a comment. It's you who turn it to an approach. Perhaps you want to be approached."

"Are you still Peter? Or is it Yuri now? Or George?"

"Peter will do."

"Thou art Peter."

Malcolm relapsed into silence, though he began to feel that it didn't matter whether he talked or not; there was something in him that was invulnerable. There was something in him that had turned to stone. The soft voice of the fire sang to him. He looked toward Peter's pale, drawn face. The man was dying.

"You look like a dying man, Peter. Why have they sent a dying man here?"

"I am an old man, but I have experience and understanding that some young men lack. I have greater depth."

He spoke without irony. Malcolm had the sense that he really believed his own words.

"Surely they didn't send you here just to talk to me. I'm of no importance."

"Your son," the man said again. Malcolm wondered if Edward's disappearance had something to do with them, if they could have taken him away.

"What about my son?"

"His actions must grieve you." They hadn't touched Edward. It was just another weapon to use against him. They broke into his house and read his mail, looking for areas of weakness, of vulnerability.

"His actions puzzle me. But I've never understood him."

"The woman wants money."

"She hasn't said that."

"Not directly."

"You are, I suppose, going to offer me money so I'll have something to give her."

Peter unclasped his hands and raised one to his head, slowly rubbing the fingers over the skin of his forehead as if to draw out the pain.

"Aren't you old enough to retire?" Malcolm said to him. "The pleasant *dacha* a few miles from Moscow, a little garden to fill your time. Why have they sent a sick man over here?"

"I have not said that I am sick."

"You don't need to say it."

The man stroked his forehead again, very slowly, returned his hand to his lap.

"Things have changed with us," he said.

"Are you in Andropov's bad books, Peter? Is this a punishment?"

Peter sat still once again, waiting, as if he had forever. He too was untouchable.

"No. It's the other way round, isn't it?" Malcolm said. "You're not here because you're in trouble. You're one of the heavyweights. An old favourite. High on the Hit Parade. But why bother with me, a church janitor? I have nothing for you. I'm an empty box."

"There are things one can do with an empty box."

"Break it apart and use it to start fires."

The man seemed suddenly now to rouse himself.

"You must be lonely here without your wife."

"Yes."

"You were the older one."

"By twelve years."

"Not to be expected that she would die first."

"No."

"She was your reason for living."

"Yes, but now I'm like other old men, I only live. I don't ask for a reason."

"Reasons are still possible."

"Working for the man who sent some Turk to kill the pope?"

"You surely don't believe that tale. Ask yourself who benefits by that story coming out? Who stands to gain by all those rumours? Why leave such an obvious trail and leave the gunman alive? We are not such fools."

"It could be said that you gain. The Polish pope has received a very clear message, and now he knows who sent the message."

"If we wanted to kill some Polish priest who flies around the world kissing the ground, he wouldn't be alive."

"Thou art Peter."

The man subsided into silence again, but now he was watching Malcolm's face, as if searching for something.

"You're here to make me a proposition," Malcolm said. "Why don't you do it?"

"I have greetings for you from a friend."

"Who?"

"Your Greek friend."

"We weren't friends, though we once agreed that in a different world we might have been."

"Have you ever asked yourself what happened in Greece?"

"I know what happened. I have the scars to prove it."

"Why it happened?"

"There were a lot of factions among the partisans who fought against the Germans, royaltists, social democrats, Communists. Nick's friends were Communists. Sometimes it wasn't easy for a Greek royalist to decide which was the greater enemy, the Germans or the reds."

"You think that's why you were betrayed?"

"It seems a likely reason."

"Have you ever thought," the man said, "that those who betrayed you might have been given orders? That there might have been a deliberate leak?"

"Why would that happen?"

"Because the British had a machine that was much more valuable than a few men. The secret to be guarded at all costs. *All costs.*"

"You're trying to tell me that they used us as protection for the machine."

"The military situation in Africa was approaching a crisis, Malcolm. You know that. The British did not believe that the Soviet workers could withstand the fascists. They thought Russia would be lost. No one had defeated the Germans on land, only the English were saved because of their Channel. Rommel was signalling from North Africa for supplies and reinforcements. To Kesselring in Rome. But each time Kesselring sent a convoy, somehow the British discovered it, and it was sunk. Because their ULTRA machine had broken the German code. Kesselring became suspicious and sent a signal to the *Abwehr* asking if there could be a leak of information about the sailing of his convoys. The *Abwehr* had no information. Kesselring was not a fool. And Rommel was not a fool. To protect their machine, the British must give the Germans a source for the information. Give the *Abwehr* a spy network to break."

"But we were in Greece, not Italy."

"Handling information about ship movements. And you weren't the only members of the network. Perhaps the network was weakened at only one spot, say a crucial one, at Naples. The Germans had to struggle for the rest of it. In the usual way."

"And we were betrayed by someone who was tortured."

"You were sent to provide a cover story for the successes of the ULTRA machine. It didn't matter how you were betrayed as long as it happened."

"They wouldn't have done that."

"They let hundreds of thousands of Soviet soldiers die to keep the machine a secret. They had information that they wouldn't give their ally because they were afraid someone might guess its source. They had many young men who were eager to work behind enemy lines. It was simple to set up a new network in the eastern Mediterranean, especially when they didn't care if the men were caught."

"But we weren't caught."

"Because the Greek Communists weren't told the secret. They got you out. No thanks to your British masters. Others were caught. And what they confessed was what the British wanted the *Abwehr* to hear."

He sat back in his chair, as if exhausted by the long story. He closed his eyes for a few moments and his breathing seemed louder. Malcolm couldn't stop the pictures from coming back. The sky and earth starting to spin as the bullets struck him. The house as Nick carried him out; it had looked like an abattoir. The little machine-gun had chopped the two Germans into pieces and scattered blood and flesh everywhere. They had left the radio behind somehow in that wild moment of escape, forgotten to destroy it. They'd sent someone back, one of the Greek Communists, but it was too late; there were more Germans there. They had received that night's British signal from Cairo.

Was that part of the plan? To send signals that would lead the Germans to the belief that the spies all through the eastern Mediterranean were more effective than they could ever possibly have been?

Was Peter's story true? Unprovable, it could be an ingenious fabrication, told to undermine his faith in his understanding of the past. A strange thing the past, as unreal as a dream. Where did it exist? Nowhere except in the mind, though historians believed that it somehow existed in the present, as a set of conditions that made a moment one particular moment, not any other.

The noise of the Sten gun was huge inside the small house. The cries of the men.

"What do you want from me?" he said to Peter. "Tell me now, straight, or leave."

The man was studying him. The skin around his eyes looked stretched and transparent, and the eyes themselves seemed to be those of a man accustomed to pain. Why had he come to Canada? Surely at his age he could have made excuses. His health was bad; they weren't going to send him to prison for being a little dilatory and demanding retirement. For some reason, he wanted to be here. Preferred to die in harness; maybe it was as simple as that.

"We need a post office," he said.

"Of course. That's how you use an empty box. You put letters in it."

"Yes."

"And within 75 miles of Ottawa. So you don't need special permission to come this far."

Peter nodded slowly. He looked bored, absent.

"Give me more details."

Peter began to rub his stiffened hand with the other. He seemed to be considering whether to go on.

"There are one or two places on your property that we would ask you to check each day. If anything is left there, you will bring it to your house and hold it for instructions. You may from time to time receive other instructions by phone or mail. All you will be required to do is to receive and sometimes to dispatch or deliver packages. Once a month, a package will be addressed to you personally. It will contain money in payment for your services."

"A regular salary. This must be important to you."

Peter relapsed into priestly silence again, waiting for the acolyte to understand a difficult theological point, or perhaps only to appreciate that he would never understand.

"How much?"

"You agree?"

"How much?"

"One hundred dollars. Each month."

"Not very much."

"Not very much is required of you."

"Show me where these drops would be."

He got up slowly from his chair and together they moved toward the door. It was a grey day, chilly, with not much sign of movement in the layers of heavy cloud. Malcolm had already guessed where the first location would be, and halfway there he stopped Peter.

"That half-dead hollow beech," he said. "That's one of them."

The other man nodded.

"You don't need to show me that."

Peter turned back toward the road. He walked with a slow, awkward, determined tread. When they were close to the road, he stopped and listened. From here it was possible to hear a car or truck coming for nearly a mile in either direction. There was no sound now except the wind in the bare branches. Peter led the way across the road. Along the edge of the road was a safety barrier of posts and wire at a point where the land suddenly dropped away, leaving a small cliff.

"You must be careful coming here," he said, "but it will be useful if it is dangerous for a car to stop."

He was right. The way the road curved, only a watcher who was right on top of the target car could see it at this point.

"You must check carefully at the bottom of the cliff."

He turned and started back to the house. Malcolm

studied the place where they were standing. A driver could slow down, drop a parcel off the edge of the road and accelerate and it would be impossible for anyone not observing him from a static post right here to know that anything had been dropped. He followed Peter back to where he stood by the door of his car.

"You will get a phone call to tell you when we are in business," he said and opened the car door.

"I haven't agreed yet."

The man nodded.

"I think you have."

The car pulled away. Malcolm stood and watched it go, and then stood still and listened to the sound of the motor becoming quieter and quieter as the car moved away from him. He turned back to the house. He was thinking about Greece, the long trip out of the hills and down to the seashore. They'd put a kind of split on his leg, two pieces of wood tied with rope, but he couldn't walk on his own. They took him part of the way on a donkey, but the donkey was as sick as he was. Then he would walk for a while, his arm over Nick's shoulder, or they would carry him. Sometimes he was feverish and confused. Finally they reached a hill over the beach, and Costas had gone down to explore. There was no moon, no light at all, and they didn't hear him coming back up, just the voice from close by.

"*I paralía íne áthia.*"

They started to make their way down the hill, Malcolm leaning on Nick so hard he was almost being carried. Not long after they reached the beach, they heard an engine over the sound of the small waves, and saw a flash of light. Again they heard a voice out of the darkness.

"*Yiá chará, Nico!*"

Costas was already on his way up the cliff. He didn't trust anyone, especially the British. It was such a complicated war, Greeks fighting the Germans and each other. The Greek civil war was already preparing itself. For a good Communist, Nick always said, it's a long war. You had to know you had history on your side. But that didn't explain why he'd chosen to save Malcolm's life. That had nothing to do with his great cause.

Malcolm had thought he was long out of those old wars.

8

Getting into the Central Registry had been easier than Borden Denny had expected. His legitimate, though thin, excuse got him a pass for headquarters and the files. He'd had a list of seven cases he wanted to consult, but he'd needed only a reference to the first; the officer in charge of the registry had agreed to let him in. Inspector Wesley, it turned out, was the classic old-fashioned Mountie in appearance, very tall, still handsome in his fifties, the kind they set in front of the parliament buildings for tourists to photograph in scarlet tunic. But Wesley appeared to be without the intense secretiveness that often went with that look, drilled into them as recruits, that they weren't like the rest of the world, that their first loyalty was always to the Force, and that the rest of the world would test that loyalty every day.

Wesley smiled broadly when Borden shook hands with him, brought to the registry by a corporal who met him at the door of headquarters.

"Figured out how to abolish us yet?" he said.

"Not yet. That's why I need your help," Borden said, trying to reply in the same tone. He'd sent a memo to McAllister to tell him he was coming here, listing most of the files he wanted and the reasons he wanted them, and he had arranged to deliver the memo and make the trip today when McAllister was out of town. By the time he read the memo, it would be done, and he would find on his desk a carbon of Borden's analysis of some of the files, with comments on their significance for the draft legislation.

But all it needed was for McAllister to decide to come back early, and to call Inspector Wesley. If he found that Borden had consulted the file on Nikos Petroff, he'd know what was up, and Denny would find himself out on his ass.

Wesley found him a table in a corner of one of the file rooms.

"Constable Richardson should be able to find what you need, Mr Denny; if there's any problem he'll just check with me, and I'm sure we can sort it out."

It was said, once again, with a broad smile, but there was a hint to it that Richardson had already received orders as to what Borden could see and what he was forbidden. He asked for three files that he was sure would present no problems. They were in the past; they'd had some public exposure, and there was no rumour of anything strange about them. He'd get Petroff's file in the second batch.

He'd left his briefcase at the entrance to the file section as they'd requested, and on the table in front of him was a plain pad of lined paper. He waited nervously for the constable to arrive back. He felt trapped here, far inside the maze of the big building, locked away, isolated in a windowless room full of paper. For all Wesley's cheerfulness, Borden knew that he was an alien here. This was a foreign country.

The constable dropped the files on the table and vanished. Borden worked through them as quickly as he could. He wanted to get to the Petroff file and through it. Once that was done, he was safe. McAllister, if he discovered him, could grumble, but nothing more.

By the time he finished reading the first three files and making notes, he was starting to get hungry, but he sent the constable back with the files he'd completed and asked for two more, one of them Petroff's. He thought the man gave him a strange look.

It was in front of him. It was safest, he'd decided, not to take notes, so he read carefully trying to digest and understand it all in a way that would keep it fresh in his mind. Most of it was familiar from the outline they'd given him in the States. Named as a Russian agent in Gouzenko's stolen papers, but without much detailed information. Vanished before he could be arrested for questioning. A number of investigative reports on his activities in Montreal before he vanished.

And a detail Borden hadn't heard before. He'd served in Greece for the British in the Second War while officially a member of the Canadian Army.

Borden took one final look through the file and closed it. He turned to the other, legitimate file and began to take notes, and when he finished he took a break for lunch. Inspector Wesley suggested they go together, and Borden concluded that all the friendship was simply another way of keeping him under control, and over lunch he was aware that he was being discreetly interrogated about the new civilian agency.

"There's going to be problems," he said to Wesley between bites of his hamburger. "Can't help but be. Your files, for example. Do we move them? Does everybody get access? Do we work in the same building?"

"Well," Wesley said, "which?"

"No idea. And it's not my problem, at least for now. Maybe McAllister can sort it out. My problem is the legislation."

"When's that going to be done?"

"I don't know."

If, by the end of the lunch, he hadn't told Wesley anything, it was less out of discretion than because there was little to tell. Setting up the new agency was laborious, and much of the planning merely technical. A million inconsequential decisions to be made, and each with a multitude of rules and regulations attached, and meanwhile Petroff's old friends were perhaps meeting somewhere in a crowded shopping centre and passing letters from hand to hand.

They drove back to RCMP headquarters and made their way to Central Registry where Borden went though the last few files, then left and drove back downtown. When he reached his office, there was a note summoning him.

"What's this all about?" McAllister said when Borden stood in front of him. He'd come back early, but not early enough.

"Just what it says."

"I'm the liaison with the Force."

"That's why I left you the memo."

"Why such a hurry? Why didn't you wait till I got back?"

"I didn't think it mattered. It was what I was prepared to do next, and I figured as long as I notified you it wasn't a big deal."

McAllister was watching him with a cool, analytic stare.

"Did you get what you wanted?" he said. There might have been a slight edge of irony to the question.

"Yes. I'll have a draft paper done tomorrow, and I'll make sure you get a copy."

"You didn't pull any extra files for your American friends while you were in there."

"No."

"I'm glad to hear it."

He sounded as if he had accepted Borden's denial.

"Why don't you put an appendix on the draft paper? A list of the files you consulted."

"I could."

"Do."

"Is there anything else?"

"Not for now."

Borden went back to his office and locked himself in. Did the Central Registry keep a record of what files were pulled and read? If so McAllister had only to compare his list with theirs to know that Borden had been reading the Petroff file. Maybe they didn't and it was just a bluff to keep him in line. He hadn't recorded the number of the Petroff file, deliberately, so it wasn't among his notes. The best thing was to list the files by number, perhaps with a deliberate mistake somewhere. No listing for Petroff. If there were one or two mistakes, that would blur the issue if McAllister decided to pursue it. How much time could he spend investigating his own men?

In the meantime, Borden had to work fanatically to have the draft paper done by the next morning. He opened his notes and began to scribble paragraphs, and late in the afternoon, he packed up all the material and took it home with him. On the way he stopped to pick up a sandwich, and with that and a bottle of beer, he continued to write. It was eleven o'clock by the time he finished, and his eyes were sore and strained. He was tired and lonely, and he wished there was a woman he could phone; he picked up the phone and dialled the first digits of Cynthia's number, but then he put it down again.

He thought of going out to a bar, but instead he opened another beer. He would get the piece typed in the morning. The next step was Petroff's army record. He wondered if McAllister had checked that when they reinvestigated the Gouzenko material.

Outside the window, flakes of snow were falling. There were fewer cars in the streets now. The snowflakes made sudden movements in the air, as if following a sequence of random impulses, and yet when you looked, not at the single flake, but at the whole air full of them, what you saw was a clear pattern of flow.

You just had to put together the pieces, and the pattern would emerge.

In the morning, he handed the draft report to Gloria, for typing. She was a large, quiet, very astute woman who had appeared from some other branch of the civil service with a high clerical rating and an unspoken disdain for most of her bosses. Borden always felt he had to explain himself to her.

"I've got a problem with McAllister over this, Gloria. It would be nice if you could do it this morning."

She counted the pages and nodded.

"If anyone's looking for me, I'll probably be over at Justice."

He wouldn't, but he assumed no one would look.

The archives of Second War army records were ancient and dusty, and so was the colonel who guarded them.

"There's a normal channel for these requests," he said, glaring from behind his desk. He had a face that was in the process of going from the red stage of alcoholism to the pale, and it seemed to be changing in blotches.

"I know there is, Colonel."

"Then why not use it?"

"This is a special case."

"The Canadian Forces don't have special cases."

"We do."

"What did you say your name was?"

"De Vries. Corporal De Vries."

"So what's so special about this case?"

"Every now and then, there's a case that we can't follow up officially because the material is too sensitive. If we can reach a certain level of proof, then we can go on with it officially."

Borden watched as the man in front of him drew

in a long breath through his wide nostrils, sucking at
the air like an addict long deprived.

"What would that mean in simple words that an
army officer could understand?"

"I can only ask you to trust me."

"Well, I don't."

There was an ominous silence. Borden was in too
far to quit now.

"It's only service records, Colonel. And you know
where I'm from."

"You people from the RCMP think you can do
whatever you want. I should have a request in writing."

His anger was turning into querulousness. He was
only being difficult because he was bored and crotch-
ety. All Borden needed to do was keep up the pressure.

"There isn't time to do it all officially."

"It sounds to me like you can't get official permission, and that's why you're poking around here on
your own."

"That situation has a number of interpretations."

"What does that mean?"

"Just what I said."

"Are you telling me that you're investigating one of
your own people?"

"No, I'm not."

"Then just what are you telling me?"

"That I need some information from Second War
service records, and I need it without an official request."

"You're very persistent."

Borden was beginning to wear him down. There was no real reason for him to deny an RCMP corporal access to the ancient records.

"It's an important matter, Colonel, or I wouldn't bother you with it. Nobody's going to know about it but you and me."

The man sniffed again, trying to build up his resistance, but it was no good. The air he breathed didn't help him.

"They can't go out of the building, you know."

"No need for that."

"I don't like this. I don't like it one bit."

"I can understand that, Colonel. The name is Petroff. Nikos Petroff."

"Sounds Russian."

"Greek."

"Sounds Russian. Probably Bulgarian originally."

He stood up and walked out of the office, and there was a long painful wait, the muttering of voices, silence. Borden moved his arms and legs which were chilled and bloodless. The seconds made their way into minutes, but in a slow, bumbling inefficient manner, while Borden wondered if the colonel was off somewhere on the phone, checking RCMP headquarters, asking about Corporal De Vries.

Voices, footsteps. The man came in, handed him a file and disappeared. Borden opened it and quickly made his way through the documents. Canada. England. Greece. Cited for gallantry. Borden read the citation. So Petroff had saved a life. He noted the name and closed the file. In the corridor outside the office, the colonel was sipping coffee with apparent distaste.

"Could I trouble you for one more file, Colonel? Same period. The name is Malcolm Fraser."

9

Never, McAllister thought, had he seen a man watch a woman's body with quite such intensity. Cliff Slater's eyes might have been prehensile organs. They didn't so much stare at the waitress's body as take a grip on it. McAllister found it embarrassing, but it would be even worse to have to tell him to stop. The girl herself was partly to blame, wearing her uniform tight and short. McAllister could see her underwear through it. He supposed she liked to be looked at, perhaps thought McAllister a fool because he didn't stare at her, imagine her naked. Cliff turned back to him.

"How are things in the upper reaches?"

"Every damn bureaucrat in sight has ten things to say that I don't want to hear. A lot of idle chatter about law and rights and politics. You're lucky that you can just get on with the job."

"We can try. They're starting to move people around. It's going to be a game of tag for the next while."

"I thought so."

"A lot of it looks the way you said. Apparently pointless movement to keep us guessing, so we don't know for a while which are the important new guys."

"A crossword puzzle."

"That's right."

Cliff's head lifted from the table to meet the waitress's approach. McAllister looked away, not to see his hungry face. It was disgusting.

"There's a couple of things I wanted to ask you," Cliff said after the girl had gone.

"Ask."

"What's going to happen to all us old cops when the new outfit gets going?"

"I think the honest answer is I don't know."

"What do you suspect?"

"There's a lot of feeling against the Force. Dumb cops, never been to school, that kind of thing. There's still some bad reaction over some of the smellier cases in Quebec. They're afraid of what the newspapers will say if the whole Security Service moves over."

"So we get the chop."

"I've only told you the one side of it. We may be dumb cops, but nobody else has any experience. They've started sending people down to the CIA to learn a few things, but that's dangerous, and if they don't already know that, they'll soon find it out. They know, deep down, that however much they may resent the Force, the public likes it and doesn't care what we did so long as we got results."

"On the one hand, on the other hand."

"That's the way they think."

"Réal says anyone with any brains should get transferred out now. Get a nice job out west where they love us."

"There's been times," McAllister said, "when I regretted I didn't do that myself."

"You don't think there's a good career in it, moving over?"

McAllister remembered the breathless discomfort every time he walked into the building, the way Borden Denny quietly defied him, never doing anything that could be punished, but always showing, somehow, that with his degrees, he held himself above a mere cop.

"Maybe I'm just too old," he said. "But there's something lousy about it. Lots of rules, but all the wrong kind. Ten forms to get paper-clips, but you can't give a man a simple order and expect him to obey."

"How about me?" Cliff said. "Would I fit in?"

"Hard to say."

"Just bull my way through, that's always been my system."

"You might just find yourself strangling in a ton of spider webs."

Cliff addressed the plate of cannelloni in front of him. He showed it the same kind of concentrated appetite that he gave the waitress's young body. McAllister looked at his own plate. He hardly felt hungry. He seemed to eat less these days. Maybe there was something wrong with him, some hidden disease, though he didn't think so, didn't believe it was that. Just that he was losing interest in things like food. He ate enough to stay alive, but beyond that it had no importance to him. He ate to live and lived to work.

"I've got to make a decision soon," Cliff said, then paused to wipe his mouth with a napkin. "Marie thinks she'd like to get out of Ottawa, so I've got to decide whether I'm going to stick with the stuff I'm doing now or pack it in."

"I wish I could help," McAllister said, "but it's all up in the air. You're going to have to gamble on it one way or the other."

"I prefer betting on sure things."

Cliff had a kind of appetite for success. McAllister himself had never been like that. His ambition had only been to fill each day with work that seemed worth doing, to do it well. Not to leave time to think about things that were better ignored. One job was the same as another, though the Security Service had an intricacy that demanded and held his concentration in a way he liked.

"You'd have to be prepared to leave the Force," McAllister said.

"Have you?"

"I'm on leave. Pension and things like that still work as if I was on the Force. I could go back, but by the time this all sorts itself out, I'll probably be forced to retire."

"Your last big fling."

"That's a godawful thought."

But it was true, of course, and McAllister hated it. This was the end, this tangle of weeds and spiders and brush. He felt like that, tied, tangled; it was probably the reason he kept thinking of the prairies, of having a little space.

"But once it's established, anyone who crosses over will be out of the Force for good."

"I expect so. When they say civilian, they seem to mean it."

"I don't understand what the difference will be."

"More nonsense and less discipline," McAllister said. "What I said before."

Cliff cleaned his plate and pushed it away.

"How long do I have to make up my mind?"

"No big hurry. By the time the legislation is drawn up and gets through Parliament and they actually start to work, we'll probably both be pensioned off."

McAllister studied his plate, wondered if he'd eaten enough to get him through the afternoon. The sight of the food revolted him, but he took a couple more bites. Cliff was looking around the restaurant, perhaps seeking another woman to assault with his eyes. He reached into his jacket, took out a picture and put it on the table facing McAllister.

"That's the second thing," he said.

McAllister studied the picture. It was a photograph taken with a telephoto lens, outside the Russian Embassy, he suspected. He couldn't see much background, but what he could see seemed familiar. The man had his head tilted a little down, as if he knew or suspected that he was being photographed and didn't want to assist the camera by looking toward it. The body was held stiffly, as if the neck or back were in pain. The face was the face of a sick man, but a man of immense discipline, who would not acknowledge the illness, who would die silently and without comment. A good enemy: McAllister studied the face. He knew what Cliff wanted from him, but he wasn't sure at first if he could provide it. He tried to let the face, the shape of the body, soak into his brain. Trust himself to find it. He waited for something. Looked at the face more closely, closed his eyes and tried to imagine the face he'd seen in front of him.

He handed the photograph back. Cliff put it away in his pocket.

"Well?"

"Nineteen forty-five," he said. "One of the cleanup men sent to patch up the damage that Gouzenko did. At least I think so. I can't be sure. He's a lot older. I know I've seen him somewhere."

"Why would he back now?"

"Hard to know. Maybe some specific job. Maybe something so touchy they need a man whose loyalty is unquestioned. Maybe something risky, so they need someone who isn't worried about the rest of his career."

"I've watched him a couple of times. He gives me the creeps."

"You're looking at a man who stood within three feet of Stalin and survived. A man who went through the war in some kind of responsible position and survived. You wouldn't want to ask what he's had to eat to do that."

"Or who?"

"That as well."

"I suppose we just do the usual with him. Watch, record, guess."

"I don't think they'd bring him back unless it was something important. He looks sick. But you know how they are. They'll spend years on a detail here, a detail there for an illegal operation, and then all of a sudden, they'll walk up to somebody at a party and openly ask him for information about espionage satellites."

"They wouldn't have sent this guy to do that."

"No. I'd guess your man — I can't remember a name and it probably wasn't his real one anyway — is doing something to set up an illegal network. Maybe using old connections who wouldn't recognize anyone else."

Slater waved to the waitress and ordered coffee. She walked away, Cliff staring.

"I said before," Cliff said, "that you shouldn't have quit. You have an instinct for these guys."

McAllister thought of the little Russian doll.

"In a way," he said, "it was like being one of them."

10

He was drowning in memory. No matter where he turned, no matter what task he set his hands to doing, the past came back, and he would find himself talking to Jean, going over things that had happened, letting her set him straight on them. The time Edward had stolen something from a store, and been caught, and had tried to keep it from them. The time Edward had wandered into the bedroom while he and Jean were making love. The period of time when Malcolm was trying to sell prefabricated houses and failing, and they had no money, sold the insurance policy, remortgaged the house, everything getting worse and worse, with Jean somehow remaining calm and helpful until the day when he came home and told her he'd taken a job at the lumber yard, and she'd stood still for a long time, while Malcolm watched her face, still so pretty, the high colour in her cheeks, and he didn't know what she was feeling as she stood there by the sink, her wet hands wrapped in her apron, and then suddenly she began to cry. He'd never seen her cry like that. She would have gone on forever waiting for him to decide that the business was hopeless, but it had been tearing her apart, and now that they had some little security, a poor job but one that was reliable, she clung to him and sobbed and held him tightly against her, and Malcolm knew there were tears in his own eyes.

The only coldness between them, ever, was over Edward. Jean, in an angry moment, told Malcolm that he was jealous of her affection for the boy, and he suspected that she was right. He couldn't share her with anyone. She was too rare.

He could see her face beside him in bed, asleep, the morning light coming through the curtains to show him the features, and he would look at her for a long time until he could look no longer, and he'd reach over and kiss her, and her eyes would open and she'd turn and hold him. When Edward was in high school, and Jean decided to get a job, he re- membered one of the men at the yard asking him if he didn't mind his wife going out to work. He had never thought that he could mind anything she did. If Jean wanted it, it must be right, and it was what he wanted too.

After lunch, he'd fallen asleep on the couch and had a dream in which she wasn't dead, and his whole body sang with relief at the realization that it was all a mistake, that they were together again, and then he had wakened, and the room was grey and cold, and he was alone. He got up from the couch and noticed that he'd left his dishes undone after lunch, and the fire had burned down to ash.

Now the fire was hot again, and he was putting

away the last of the dishes and trying to forget the dream. He couldn't bear to think of how happy he had felt. Jean alive. With him. He mustn't think such things, not even in dreams.

He walked to the front window and stared out toward the woods across the road. There was a light dust of snow on the rust and umber carpet of dead leaves, and the trunks and branches wove together into a hypnotic pattern.

Margaret had invited him for dinner, and he had agreed to go, but now he didn't care to, not in this state of mind. He might say or do anything.

Malcolm could still remember the first time he had seen the woman who would be his wife. It was an unromantic moment, at a party to which she'd come with Tom McAllister, just as everyone was leaving, and she was bending down to fasten her galoshes. They were high and narrow, with fur around the top, and Malcolm hardly noticed her there in the crowded hallway, until she stood up, and her face, from the heat in the house, the excitement of the party, the effort of bending to fasten the boots, was flushed and bright, and their eyes met, only for a second, and he walked home wondering who she was, whether she had felt anything in that moment.

He thought sometimes, with a kind of terror, that he might never have seen her again. Things like that happened. People you saw once only. What would his life have been if they hadn't met again and been introduced? Jean might have married Tom McAllister. And Malcolm?

It had been a dangerous time for him, right after the war, the wounds still fresh. He might have gone under if it hadn't been for Jean's love. She led him through it all.

Unfortunate. That was the word that Peter had used about her death. Unfortunate. What a dreary word.

He saw a flash of movement among the trunks of the bare trees. A jay. This far away he couldn't hear its raucous cry.

On the ground in front of the house lay the dead bodies of the clump of peonies that Jean had planted. He could see her there, the shovel in her hand, wearing a pair of his old work gloves as she separated a clump of tubers, like thin cancerous potatoes, setting them in place and covering them. She was wearing one of his old jackets. He liked it when she wore his clothes for gardening or a walk in the woods, and in fact she did it, not because she had nothing else to wear, but as a gesture of love.

He must stop this, smarten himself up before he went to have dinner with Margaret. He wasn't sure that he could keep up his end conversationally; something about Margaret silenced him, at times. When he looked at her no words came. They were both lonely, and company was welcome to each, but it wasn't that simple. Malcolm was aware of being polite.

Spoiled. He'd never had to think, with Jean, what he ought to say. Words came, or silence, and it didn't matter.

He had seen her dead, in the hospital, and again at the funeral home. He'd gone to the hospital, begging God or fate that there might be a mistake, that the body would be a stranger, but the pale, empty face with the mouth hanging a little open was the face he loved, and he didn't know whether he wanted to scream and run, or whether he wanted to seize the body and hold it to him to warm it, to bring it back to life. He touched the skin of her face with his fingers; he kissed the forehead and then he turned and walked out of the hospital, drove to the house, loaded the rifle and walked into the woods. It was early spring, the leaves just beginning to unfold, and the first insects buzzed around him; he walked until he was lost in the trees, and it was only then he fully realized that he had come to kill himself.

He wasn't sure now why he hadn't.

He had to see her through the rest of it, partly that. He wouldn't abandon her body to strangers.

He'd returned to the house and unloaded the gun. He'd gone through the days without thought, as if the moment in the woods with the gun were waiting for him, making him calm, giving him peace, as if he'd already put the gun in his mouth and pulled the trigger, and all the rest of this was a dream that he had to complete before oblivion would come.

But he'd stayed alive. He didn't know why. It had, somehow, a connection with Greece, with having survived when it seemed he was marked for death. A man whose life has been saved by other men no longer possesses it wholly. He isn't in his own hands.

Once in the early days of marriage, as he lay in bed, Jean in his arms asleep after making love, he had thought of this as a gift that Nick had given him. The happiness of private life that Nick himself would despise. Politics, Malcolm had once said to him, on a sunny Greek afternoon, ought to serve living. Petit-bourgeois, Nick had mumbled. Petit-bourgeois.

Another sudden flash of colour in the woods. The jay again. The sun as it moved down in the sky had appeared at the edge of the clouds, and was shining across the trees, sudden spots of rich light appearing here and there. The woods went on for miles, dim and quiet, with these spots of golden late sun gleaming unseen.

Malcolm turned from the window and, after checking the stove and adding some wood, went to the bedroom to change. He wasn't sure whether he ought to dress up for his dinner visit. He'd never seen Margaret in anything but the old clothes she usually wore, but she must have others. She surely didn't wear those when she attended church.

On the table by the bed was a picture of Edward and his family that Jean had asked them to send her. Malcolm picked it up and looked carefully at the four figures. They were sitting at a picnic table somewhere, and he could see the mountains in the background. Edward stood a little away from the other three, as if he didn't want to be taken for one of them. How long had he shut himself away? The woman was smiling, but the smile was fugitive, as if it were only a mask for her tears. The boy's smile seemed real. The little girl was ignoring the camera, all her attention on something outside the picture.

Edward stood to one side, as if he were already shifting away from the family, moving toward the margin, ready to slip away. With his thumb, Malcolm covered the figure of his son and then it was a picture of the three that were left. On the dresser nearby lay

Connie's letter. Malcolm knew it by heart, and phrases from it might come into his mind during the day and sadden him. *Most men don't just leave and not get in touch.* Even her anger was muted and sorrowful. He looked at Frank's smiling face and thought how lonely the boy must be. There should be things Malcolm could do. He'd written, sent some money, promised to send more.

He looked again at Edward's figure, cool, mysterious. *He has behaved badly,* Peter had said, Peter, who had broken into the house, looking for things to use against him. *His actions must grieve you.* Grief. There was too damn much grief.

Malcolm stripped off his clothes and stepped into the shower. His leg was aching, and the hot water eased it a little. When he was out of the shower and dry, he wiped the steam off the mirror and shaved the worn, rather severe face that stared at him. Perhaps he'd been cold with Edward, too hard on him. But Jean had loved the boy, and she was good at it, good at loving. *He has behaved badly.*

It was nearly dark when Malcolm drove down the road toward Margaret's house. Malcolm stood at the door for a long time, the bottle of wine in his hand, until at last she arrived, a thin, ungainly figure in a maroon dress that looked as if it had been resurrected from some party in the distant past. But she looked younger, as if she had gone back to the year the dress was in style.

"I brought some wine."

"Oh good. That will be a treat. I'm not much of a drinker. Always been afraid I'd get to like it and turn into a sot."

"I can't imagine that," Malcolm said.

He hung his coat on the ornate hall tree by the door.

"Oh I can. Sherry at bedtime and toppling into bed. Just the thing for an old maid."

She led the way into the living-room; it was crowded with furniture, some of it antique and elegant, much of it just out of date. Against one wall were three stacks of magazines and on a small desk lay a pile of envelopes and church circulars, with various pens and pencils and the kind of ink bottle Malcolm remembered from school.

"It seems odd to leave you here all alone while I finish cooking the dinner," Margaret said, "but I suppose it's proper."

"Why don't I just come out to the kitchen like old friends?"

"Yes, that is a better idea, isn't it?"

She led the way through the dining-room, where a coloured glass lampshade hung on a chain over the table, a dim bulb inside. On the table was an ancient lace tablecloth, a little yellowed with age and disuse. They made their way into the kitchen, which was even more disorderly than the last time Malcolm had been in it. There was a pleasant smell of roasting meat, and the room was warm and a little steamy.

"I'm not a fancy cook, Malcolm, as you might have guessed. But I can manage the basics."

She looked for a place to put down the wine bottle, and when she couldn't find one, passed it back to him.

"Why don't you open it? Do you need a corkscrew? I don't think we have one."

"I have one on this knife," Malcolm said. He took out the red Swiss Army knife.

"That's very bright and shiny," Margaret said.

"Edward's family sent it to me last Christmas. All the young people carry them. I always find it a bit embarrassing."

He took out the corkscrew and opened the bottle. Margaret brought two juice glasses to him.

"I don't have wine glasses, I'm afraid."

Malcolm filled the two glasses. She raised hers.

"To all the lonely old church mice," she said.

Her face, usually pale, was a little flushed from the heat of the kitchen, and perhaps from some exertion or excitement. As he looked at the disorder of the room around him, the vegetable peel still in a pile on the counter, a bag of groceries half-unpacked on the table, Malcolm felt a desire to tidy, but he sipped the wine and tried to ignore it. Awkwardly, Margaret drained the roast and began trying to skim the fat off the juice. She was all thumbs, and it seemed cruel to be watching her.

"Have you seen anyone else behaving suspiciously around the church?" he said. He thought immediately it was a stupid question to ask, but he'd needed to say something, and he'd unwittingly spoken his mind.

"Last week," she said. "Why?"

"No reason."

"You're being mysterious again."

"No. Just making conversation. I'm out of practice."

"No more so than I am. Too many days spent talking to myself."

She was stirring flour into the gravy. The way she threw in more, Malcolm felt sure it was going to be lumpy. He drank more wine and wondered who she'd seen at the church. Maybe she was imagining things. Or maybe it was Peter back. Or someone working for Peter. He wondered still why they'd sent the old man back. They must have something planned.

That story of how he and Nick were to be sacrificed deliberately, to prevent the Germans from knowing that their ciphers were being broken: was it true? Things like that had happened in France; men sacrificed to ensure surprise for the Normandy landings. That was what war was about. You sent men to be killed to gain some territorial or logistic advantage. But the men were told. In the secret wars no one was told the truth. Maybe never knew it.

"Why don't you take the wine in to the table?" Margaret said.

Malcolm did as he was bidden and she followed with a small overcooked roast on a plate.

"If you want to carve," she said, "I'll bring in the vegetables."

As Malcolm sliced the meat, bowls arrived with potatoes, carrots, and frozen peas. She set them down and took her place opposite him.

"Do you mind," she said, "if I say grace?"

"No," he said, "of course not."

He sat in silence while she spoke the words, and then they both raised their heads and helped themselves to the food.

"I've been worrying," she said, "about these people watching you."

"Probably we're both imagining them," he said.

"Dotty old church mice."

"Yes."

He ate a few mouthfuls of food from his plate. Margaret ate carefully, as if she had trouble with her teeth or digestion, and after a few mouthfuls, she put down her fork.

"We're not, are we?"

"What?"

"Dotty. Imagining them."

"I don't know. We could be."

Again, she ate a few small bites.

"How did it happen?" she said, "you becoming a secret agent in Greece."

"I don't know quite how they picked me. I had some radio training. I'd been in the RCMP and done undercover work when I first joined."

"You're full of mysteries."

"There's nothing mysterious or fine about undercover work. You just tell lies."

"You wouldn't be good at that, would you?"

"I managed well enough. I didn't like it."

"Why did you do it?"

"I was a new recruit, straight off the farm. When they said jump, I jumped."

"You sound almost bitter."

"No, I don't think so, not bitter, but things are different when you look back."

"Yes, they are."

Her voice sounded sad, and she turned to the food on her plate, proceeding through it with the same small careful bites, eating as she had been taught to eat, he supposed.

"If there's anything I'm bitter about," he said, "it's losing Jean."

"She was a lovely person, Malcolm. When I heard you were going to be the new sexton, I was sure I'd like you because of her. She was such a nice person, and happy. I knew that her husband must be a good man."

"He did his best."

Silence seemed to take them then, as if the house fell suddenly into the hands of its ghosts, as if the whole world, perhaps, fell suddenly into the grip of the past, and the spirits of the dead did all the talking.

11

Borden Denny stood on the steps of the public library and looked down the narrow street of this dim northern Ontario town toward the cluster of stores that made the business district of the place. Most of them looked pretty unsuccessful. It was a dead end. The motel where he'd taken a room had cracks in the plaster and towels that looked as if they'd been washed too often.

He walked down the steps and turned toward the newspaper office to see if he could find anyone who'd remember the riot. The old newspaper reports he'd read in the library didn't tell him what he needed to know. On the corner was a restaurant with video games at the front. A girl in tight jeans was playing one of them.

Between the restaurant and the newspaper office was a bare-looking health-food store; shelves of unfinished wood and bins of fruit and nuts.

The sign outside the newspaper office was ancient. The Review. Job Printing, Personal and Commercial.

It was a dead-end town, for sure. The front window still had the old wooden mullions between the panes. When Borden opened the door, he could hear the rhythmic sound of the presses working somewhere in the back of the building. The young woman at the desk behind the counter had a pale, fat face. She smiled.

"Would there be anyone here," Borden said, "who might have worked on the paper in the 1930s."

"Mr Lyall would be the only one. I don't really know when he started. I just been here a couple of years."

"Is he a reporter?" Borden recognized the name.

"He's the publisher. He owns the paper."

She bobbed her head every time she made an assertion as if to help it on its way, to assert her own agreement to whatever you thought of it.

"I'd like to talk to him."

"He's in his office right now, working on an editorial. I guess I could take you along and see."

She nodded again, stood and came out from behind the counter. She was wearing high heels that made her move with an unnatural lumbering gait.

She led Borden down a narrow hall to a solid wooden door. She knocked.

"It's Myrna, Mr Lyall. There's a man here would like to talk to you."

The door opened. Lyall was a man of medium height with a smooth, pleasant face, straight hair, still thick though almost white. He wore a dress shirt and tie, but the sleeves of the shirt were rolled up. His air was clerical and astute.

"What can I do for you?"

"Are you the Ernest Lyall who wrote the stories about the riot in the relief camp here in the thirties?"

"That's right."

"Could you spare me a few minutes?"

"I think so. Come in. We'll let Myrna get back to her desk."

Borden entered the room and Lyall closed the door behind him.

"Why don't you sit down over there?"

Borden sat in the wooden armchair that was offered to him.

"I've been at the library reading your stories about the riot."

"I suppose it wasn't much of a riot by today's standards, but we were all pretty worried at the time."

"Did you meet any of the organizers?"

"I was right inside the camp. They seemed to think I'd tell the truth, so they let me in even when they locked out the police."

"Who were the organizers among the men?"

Borden wondered if he was pushing too fast, but he knew what he wanted, and he hadn't the patience to wait forever to get to the point.

"Agitators," the man said. "That's what they called them in those days. Communist agitators. I don't suppose you'd know what it was like in the Depression."

"That's why I'm asking you to tell me."

"I was pretty young myself then."

He stopped and studied Borden, calmly and carefully.

"What's your interest in all this?" he said.

"I'm writing a book," Borden said.

"I suppose you might find some of the men who

were in the camp. They were mostly pretty young then. Your age or younger. Mostly from the cities. Single and unemployed. Put them to work cutting timber for twenty cents a day."

"And the riot," Borden said. "How did that happen?"

"They started a union in the camp. In a bunch of the camps. The Relief Camp Workers' Union. It was all secret. If they found out the men who were organizing it, they arrested them as agitators. The police had spies in all the camps."

"Did you meet any of the police spies?" Borden said.

The man gave a little sniff that was a kind of laugh.

"They didn't announce themselves. I had my suspicions. So did the men. It was a long time ago. What I remember best is the feeling in the camp, what it's always been like when you get a bunch of men together, but bitter. Rough and crude and bitter."

"The march into town," Borden said. "Who organized that?"

"There was a secret committee. I knew who they were, but I agreed that if they let me into the camp I wouldn't talk to the police. They never came right out and told me who they were, but I pretty well knew."

"Do you remember any of them now?"

"There was a Greek fellow I think was the ringleader. I remember that because there weren't many Greeks. Mostly Ukrainians and Poles, the foreigners."

Borden made himself wait, breathe slowly. He'd

found it, the connection he'd known must be there. It was going to work out.

"Do you know his name, this Greek?"

"Not any more. A Greek name."

"Would you recognize a picture of him?"

Borden had found a picture in one of the newspapers from the time of the Gouzenko investigation. It was old and blurred, a poor quality newspaper reproduction, but it might be enough. He held it out to Ernest Lyall, who took it and then put it down on his desk, as if he didn't want to be seen touching it.

"It looks familiar," he said, "but I'd hate to commit myself. It's more than forty years ago. How'd you get the picture?"

"Part of my research."

Lyall handed the picture back.

"Did I get your name?" he said.

"De Vries," Borden said. "Fred De Vries."

Lyall patted himself on the cheek a few times with his fingertips, as if to remind himself of something.

"I tell you, Mr De Vries," he said. "If you're going to go around pretending to be a writer, you'd better do some more work on the part. You're not very good at it. Writers ask a different kind of question."

Borden didn't care any more what the man thought of him. He had what he wanted.

"You can't remember the man's name."

"No."

"Does Petroff sound familiar? Nikos Petroff?"

Lyall tapped his cheek again.

"I couldn't swear to it, but I think that's the name of the man who was on the committee. Is he in some kind of trouble?"

"He's dead," Borden said.

"I suppose it's all history now. I guess somebody should write a book about it while there's a few of us around that remember the bits and pieces."

He stood up from his desk.

"I'd better get back to my editorial on the Simcoe Street potholes. It's a pressing topic."

Lyall held out his hand and Borden shook it. It was a dry warm hand, smooth and muscular.

Borden left the office, nodded to the pale, round face of Myrna at the front desk and made his way back to the street. Petroff had been in the camp. Borden had learned from RCMP records that Fraser had been in the camp as a police spy. Another connection between them. It was all there. How much of it did Bud Hurnick already know when he started Borden on the trail? Was it just an exercise, to let him discover things they already knew? He couldn't believe that. How would any of them have got access to the RCMP and army records?

Borden walked down the street toward the motel where he had left the car.

12

Margaret shivered. The world outside was a block of ice, and inside, where she kept the thermostat low to save fuel, it was almost as bad.

She was watching the church. Malcolm's car was parked outside, but soon, she thought, it would be time for him to leave for lunch. It was foolish, she knew, to stand at the window like this, just to see him coming and going, but somehow it did her good. And there was always the chance that she might see one of the strange cars that had appeared once or twice to observe the church, to wait for him.

What wouldn't she be imagining next? Making herself into some kind of secret agent. Why would anyone be spying on a decent old widower who worked as a church sexton? Next thing she'd be reporting to the police that strange men were staring at her, or that there were voices in her attic. She could see a police officer, nodding, taking down the details, turning to a colleague after she left and tapping his head.

Still, she hadn't entirely lost her mind, not yet, and

119

she was determined, the next time she saw a car driven by a stranger and behaving oddly, that she would stop it or at least write down the licence. If she got a licence number, Malcolm would know what to do with it. He had, she suspected, friends and associates in important positions who could help him.

She saw him now, as he came out the door of the church hall and moved down the walk toward his car, and she felt happy, just to have seen him, to know he was in the world, and the pathos of her own happiness brought tears to her eyes. She was a pathetic old bag. She drew back from the window a little lest he look up and see her there.

Malcolm's life, his marriage to Jean, that was the way life was supposed to work, not this dull solitude of regret.

The car drove away and she moved forward to watch it until it was out of sight. He was gone. Into some other world. Sometimes Margaret tried to imagine his life, the reasons the men watched him, the secrets, important, weighty, that still involved him. Jean must have known about them. Margaret never could. There would never be anything between them but the careful friendship that they had created. She mustn't try to grab for more or she would make him uncomfortable. If she let herself be satisfied to see him at the church, perhaps now and then to invite him for coffee or maybe, once in a long while, for dinner, then he wouldn't be frightened away, and her life would be warmed by knowing that he was nearby.

It was better than before he'd come to the church, and she knew she must thank God for what she had, rather than demand more. If Margaret could have sacrificed herself to bring Jean back to him, she would have; there was little enough of her, of her life, to give, but since God had decreed Jean's death, Margaret would allow herself the pleasure it had brought to her.

She was shivering harder now. She would dress warmly and take a brisk walk downtown.

13

Borden Denny stepped on the gas to move the car more quickly toward its destination, all the while knowing that if there was a big mistake to be made this could be it. It was dangerous to confront Fraser, but somehow he had to see him. The documents had told him a lot, but now that he'd found Fraser he needed to see the man's face, to hear his voice. He had to take the case another step or two farther before he passed it on.

How was he going to do that? It was a puzzle. McAllister would give him no points for pursuing the matter, only a dressing down for disobeying him. To pass the information to the Americans would get him something, but it would, as McAllister had warned, put him in their pocket, and in the long run he could only lose by that. The only thing to do was to push the case as far as he could and then go over McAllister's head with it, go to someone who wasn't from the RCMP and might be less rigid.

He would have to trust his luck. The last few years,

his luck had been good; things fell right for him. When Borden finished law school, he had looked around him at the career possibilities and wondered if the whole thing had been a mistake. Legal practice in some small city wasn't very appealing; most places you'd want to live already had too many lawyers. You'd grind out wills and mortgages and divorces, maybe an interesting piece of litigation every five years. And that was it. He'd never had the connections or the kind of brilliance to see him into a good corporate position. He could, perhaps, have made his way into a small company and worked his way up, but the odds were high.

He'd been planning to go to Peterborough, his eyes sharp for something better, when the chance came to article with the provincial ministry of justice. When he went there, he knew that he had opened the right door. Borden had always possessed a gift for organization, back to the days when he had saved high-school charitable projects that were about to collapse, and he liked the kinds of issues involved in government work. The rumours about how little civil servants worked were, in his experience, not true, and even the amount of red tape wasn't much worse, he gathered from friends, than what arose in any big corporation. Government was big business, and big business was complicated. He had decided to work in government, and after he finished the Bar Admissions course he found a position with the feds and moved to Ottawa.

Since then, things had gone well. Being drafted onto the planning staff for the new security service was a sign that he was regarded as a comer. In a new

organization, it was possible to move a lot faster than
in the established programs of an established ministry. The interest the Americans had shown in him
was flattering. They thought it worth while to court
him, to try to draw him into some kind of secret alli-
ance with them. They were dangerous partners, but
they weren't small-time.

He slowed the car to go down a steep curving hill,
turn at the bottom and start up another, even
steeper. The road was clear of snow, but there were
patches lying in the pale woods. The sky was overcast,
and though it was early in the afternoon, night felt
close by. He'd driven this way on the weekend, made
sure that he knew where Fraser's house was, found a
place to leave his car that was close, but out of sight of
the house; Borden didn't want Fraser recording his
licence number. If he was still working for the Russians, they could find a way of tracing it. But he
thought Fraser might believe the cover story he had
to offer.

It would be an advantage to work through this on
his own. Otherwise he'd be in the same position as so
many of the other civilians, having to accept what the
Mounties told them or know nothing. There was a
strong suspicion among those developing the new security program in the Solicitor-General's department
that the RCMP Security Service meant to move in the
whole outfit, put their dress uniforms in mothballs,
and go on in just the way they had before. There had
been civilian heads of the Security Service, but their
power was always circumscribed by the cohesiveness
of the RCMP loyalty. If Borden could run down an
RCMP failure and set up a working relationship with

the Americans, he'd be in an excellent position, especially if he could work round McAllister. McAllister wouldn't be there much longer anyway; he was near retirement age.

He was driving the last stretch of road before Fraser's house. He felt himself on edge, but tried to think of it as nothing more than a minor court appearance, a kind of cross-examination. He'd once done a particularly good cross-examination in his first moot court appearance; there was no reason not to handle this. Fraser was the one with something to fear, not Borden Denny.

The car slid off the main road onto the worn track of a logging trail into the woods. He got out and walked along the edge of the road to the driveway that led to Fraser's house. It was a small, neatly kept place. By asking a few questions around the town, Borden had learned that Fraser was a widower living alone, so it was unlikely there would be anyone else around. The car was parked at the side of the house beside a neat stack of firewood.

Borden walked to the door.

The man who answered had a rifle in his hands, and for a moment, Borden was shaken.

"Don't look so nervous about the gun," the man said. "I was about to go out hunting."

"Are you Malcolm Fraser?"

"That's right."

"I was hoping to talk to you."

"Come in, then. We'll give the birds a few more minutes of life."

He leaned the gun against the wall, then closed the door behind Borden. In the corner a woodstove radiated heat. Borden tried not to be caught watching, but he couldn't escape being fascinated that this man had been a secret agent in Greece, that he had warned Petroff that he was named in Gouzenko's documents, that he might, even now, be an active Russian agent. Fraser looked toward him.

"My name's De Vries," Borden said, "Fred De Vries."

"Why don't you sit down, Mr De Vries, and tell me what I can do for you?"

Borden sat on a couch upholstered in dark blue corduroy. Fraser settled in a chair near the stove.

"I'm a journalist," Borden said, "freelance."

Fraser only nodded. Borden found it hard to go on without garbling the words. He made himself speak slowly.

"I'm working on a story," he said, "about Canadians who were involved in undercover work during the Second World War."

"Why did you come to see me?"

"I believe you were one of them."

"What gave you that idea?"

"I've done a lot of research."

"I'm sure you have," Fraser said. Borden couldn't quite make out the tone of the remark, how much irony there was in it.

"Tell me what you've learned," Fraser said.

"You were infiltrated into Greece in 1942. You were there for several months. You were wounded and taken out."

"That's right."

"I was hoping you'd tell me about it in a little more detail."

"That would be a long story, wouldn't it?"

"I'm patient," Borden said. He was more comfortable now. He was beginning to almost believe his own lie about being a journalist.

"What sort of thing did you want to know?"

"Tell me about Nikos Petroff."

"I was his pianist."

Borden looked at him to see if it was some kind of joke.

"I don't quite follow," he said.

"Well, Mr De Vries," Fraser said, "there's a piece of research you missed. I was his radio operator. We were called pianists because we sent Morse code with our fingers, and we had to be very fast."

"It's foolish of me not to know that," Borden said. He took a pad and pencil out of his pocket and made a note.

"Well, now you know," Fraser said.

"So you were sent into Greece as a radio operator for Petroff. He spoke Greek, I suppose."

"That's right."

"Did you?"

"He taught me a few phrases."

The man sat in his place on the other side of the room, one hand on each arm of the chair. He seemed perfectly composed, fatalistic. Without asserting himself in any way, he gave the impression that he, not Borden, was in control of this interview.

"How were you wounded?" Borden said.

"The Germans shot me."

"But you escaped."

"Yes."

"I'd like you to tell me about it. How they found you. How you escaped."

"It's not a story I usually tell people. I don't know why. I don't suppose any of it's secret any more. We were betrayed by someone. I never knew who it was, though I think Nick had some ideas. He knew a lot more about politics than I did. I looked after radio, transport, all the mechanics of our communication with the British bases in North Africa."

"How did you escape?"

"We were careful. Nick was a good agent, meticulous and brave. The Germans came straight to the house. Someone had told them just where to come. Nick was away, and I saw them in time to make a break for it. That's when I was shot. But there was a pile of rocks behind the house, a sort of cairn. It didn't look like anything very significant, but it was a signal to anyone coming to the house. If it was broken or rearranged in any way, something was wrong. As I was running, I managed to knock it down. The Germans took it as an accident, a wounded man falling on some rocks. But the cairn was placed so it could be seen from a long way back up the path, before you were visible from the house. They kept me in the house, waiting for Nick to come back, but he saw the broken cairn."

"He set you free."

"He carried me I don't know how far through the hills, hid me for the night and got in touch with one of the partisan groups. They got us to a safe place on the shore, and we were picked up."

Fraser had told the story without moving. He still

sat in exactly the same position in the chair. He might have been talking in his sleep.

"Petroff saved your life."

"That's right."

Borden made a few notes on his pad, what a journalist would have needed to remember the story.

"Have you heard from Petroff recently?" he said.

"No. I don't know where he is. It's been a long time."

"When did you come back to Canada?"

"Not long after that. I was sent back to recuperate and Nick became an instructor for other men who were going in behind German lines."

"Was Petroff a Communist?"

"Yes. So were a lot of the Greek partisans. We always thought that was what got us betrayed to the Germans. Groups fighting among themselves."

"Had you ever met Petroff," Borden said, "before you were sent to Greece together?"

Borden wasn't sure how far to go, where to stop, but the questions were there, and now that he was with Fraser, it seemed, he might as well ask them.

"We were trained together, in England."

"I meant before that."

"Why would you think we'd met before that?"

"Just an idea, something that came up in my research."

The cloudy sky cleared for a moment and a beam of sun shone through the window and lit Fraser's hand and arm. The veins and cords on the back of his hand stood out.

"You tell me what you have in mind," Fraser said, and again Borden had the disquieting feeling that

Fraser was in control of this interview, that he was calm and sure and unfrightened.

"A relief camp in northern Ontario," Borden said. "There was some kind of demonstration. A small riot. People from the camp marched to the town."

"And?"

Borden stepped over the line.

"According to my information, you were one of the men in the camp. You were an RCMP informer."

For the first time, Fraser turned and looked at him.

"You must be a good writer, Mr De Vries. With your sources of information."

"I'm persistent. When I want some information I just keep digging till I get it."

"Yes, I suppose you would."

Borden felt a need to get control of this interview, to shake Fraser out of his complacency.

"Petroff's dead," he said.

Fraser didn't show any sign of shock.

"Is he?" he said.

"He died in Greece a few weeks ago."

Fraser was silent, waiting.

"When was the last time you saw him?" Borden said.

"I suppose it was sometime just after the war."

"What were you doing then?"

"With your persistence in research, I'm sure you must know."

He was no longer looking at Borden, just sitting back in the chair, his eyes on something distant.

"Was this after you'd gone back to the RCMP?" Borden said. He was giving himself away, but perhaps it didn't matter. If Fraser were to confess, he could go to McAllister and drop the whole thing on his desk. What McAllister had failed to find, Borden had found.

"I went back as soon as my leg was strong enough to convince them I wasn't a cripple."

"Petroff was named in the papers that Gouzenko took from the Russian embassy, wasn't he? As one of the Russian agents operating in Canada."

"His name's right there in the report of the Royal Commission."

"But he was never arrested."

"They couldn't find him."

Borden couldn't understand why Fraser didn't seem more shaken. Nothing he said seemed to touch the man. No matter how hard he pushed.

"I wonder how he knew enough to escape?" Borden said.

"When we were in Greece, we used to talk about how you sensed danger. Nick used to claim that he had a third eye, right in the forehead, and when it started to see things, he knew there was trouble coming. And when he saw trouble, it didn't take him long to act. That's why I'm still alive."

"You must have felt grateful toward him."

"Grateful is a small, mean word."

His tone annoyed Borden. Fraser thought he was untouchable.

"Did you have access to the work of the Gouzenko investigation?" Borden said.

Fraser got up from his chair and walked past Borden to the window.

"That's a good question for a persistent hard-working writer like you to have a go at," Fraser said. "By

the look of the light, there's about an hour till dark.
If I'm lucky I might still be able to pick a partridge
out of a tree. They settle down for the night. I guess
they think they've got through another day of the
hunting season successfully, and then I come
through the woods. They have a moment of worry at
the sound or the smell of me, and then the lights go
out. I'm a good shot."

Borden wondered if it was some kind of warning.
He stood up, put away his pencil and pad, began to
button his coat.

"Thank you for answering my questions," he said.
"You've been a big help."

"Writing isn't my line of country," Fraser said. "I
wouldn't know much about it."

"Maybe we can talk again some time," Borden said
as he moved to the door.

"Well, Mr De Vries, I think I'd like the past to stay
in the past." He paused for a moment and spoke
again. "One thing you could tell me."

"Yes."

"Nick. According to your information, how did he
die?"

"Natural causes. He got sick and died."

Borden opened the door and left.

Malcolm stood at the window for some time after the
man had gone, then took down his jacket, which
hung on a rack behind the door. He picked up the
.22. There was a package of cartridges in the pocket
of his jacket, and as he walked along the path into the
woods, he loaded the rifle. There was a bit of breeze,

the particular quiet sound of wind in bare branches. As he made his way through the trees, his eyes saw the dark colours of the early winter, the occasional pale patches of snow here and there, but they saw these things in a way that was only automatic; the familiarity of every step was soothing, but he was far away from it as well.

He wouldn't have thought that the news of Nick's death would be such a shock. It was more than thirty years since they'd met. Malcolm thought back to the young man who'd given him the information, the handsome unappealing face.

Who would be the next one to arrive? And with what news?

Perhaps it wasn't true, the story of Nick's death. The man had told him lies, Malcolm knew that.

He made his way on through the woods until he came to a clearing on the side of a hill where a large chunk of granite was thrust into the air from beneath the roots of a large, half-hollow beech. He sat down on the piece of rock. There had been no sign of birds in the woods, but he didn't much care. His mind was away, somewhere else. In Greece maybe. In the past.

This was the spot he had come to with the gun after he had seen Jean's dead body. It was here he'd planned to kill himself. What was it had brought him back today, after the news that Nick was gone? Nick wasn't even a friend, really. Something else. But the news of his death made Malcolm feel more alone. He couldn't bring himself to care much who this De Vries was, why he was telling lies, what he was after. It didn't seem to matter. None of it mattered.

Still, he wasn't ready to let go. Not yet. He'd had a

letter from Connie the day before, thanking him for the last money he'd sent, and enclosing a note from his grandson. The girl was too young to write yet. He wanted to get to Vancouver to see them. He wanted to help them make something of their lives, even without Edward.

He wondered if Nick had children living, grand-children. He'd never shown much enthusiasm for do-mestic life, despised it mostly, but once he was back in Greece it would have been natural enough for him to marry.

Life and death; they seemed both obvious and mysterious now that he was old. People vanished, and yet inside you, in your mind, they went on.

Once more he examined the words that De Vries had said, looking for the meaning, looking for the lies. Once more he concluded that about Nick at least he was right, or believed he was. The man who'd given Malcolm back his life was dead.

Darkness was closing in on the woods, darkness and cold. When he got back to the house, he'd write to Connie and include a letter for the boy. He'd found the feather of a jay the other day, bright blue. He'd include that. Frank would like it.

As he stood to return to his house he thought again of Nikos Petroff, the powerful ugly face empty. Dead.

"*Yiá chará*, Nico," he said. He said it aloud, to the rocks and the trees, to whatever was.

14

*M*alcolm sat at a table in the corner of the pub and watched the strong white arm of the barmaid as she pulled pint after pint of draught beer. The flesh on her arms was heavy, a creamy white colour mottled a little with pale pink. In front of her, a tall heavy man, his cheeks purple with broken veins, was delivering a diatribe on desert warfare.

There was little chance of bombs this far out in the country, but every now and then there would be a distant drone of aircraft, and a momentary shift upward of the eyes of someone in the room. Malcolm was drinking alone, but he suspected that there was someone watching him. So far, they hadn't told him what this training was all about, though there couldn't be much doubt. He'd been selected for special training for one of the irregular forces that were attempting to harass the Germans as a prelude to an invasion. He could tell by the rhythm of the training that they were going through some kind of preliminary selection; those who were picked would go on to something more intensive.

He drained his pint of bitter and went back to the bar for

*another. The barmaid smiled with professional cheerfulness
and pulled him a pint.*

"There you go, Canada," *she said, and he pushed the
coins across to her. He hadn't drunk much, only enough to
be reminded that he was away from home, and that this
country they were fighting to defend seemed foreign to him.
He went back to his table, and as he lifted the pint of beer to
his mouth the man appeared in the doorway, the Greek who
was also part of the special training scheme. They had recognized each other, but they hadn't spoken. Now the man
walked to the bar and ordered a whisky. He drank it and ordered another.*

*Malcolm looked around the room trying to work out who
it was must be observing them. They'd been allowed to leave
the house where the training was going on and come into
town for the evening, but the reasons weren't, he was sure,
humanitarian ones. It was a way of learning something
about them.*

*A man and woman stood at the end of the bar. The
woman was tall and plain, wore a blue skirt and jacket.*

*The man, the Greek, was standing beside his table. Mal-
colm gestured to the chair. The man hesitated, then sat
down.*

"You remember?" *he said abruptly.*

Malcolm nodded.

"Not the name," *Malcolm said.*

"Petroff," *he said.* "Nick Petroff."

"Malcolm Fraser."

*The woman by the bar had put herself in a position where
she could see them without having to look. Malcolm glanced
around the room to see if any of the other men from the
group at the large country house were there, but he could see
none.*

"You were lucky to get out of that relief camp alive," Petroff said to him.

"Why is that?"

"You know how the men in the camp felt about informers."

Malcolm didn't answer.

"You betrayed them," Petroff said.

"I was sent there to do a job."

"You were sent?"

"The first thing I was assigned to do after I finished my RCMP training."

"A cop," Petroff said. "A traitor to your class."

"I didn't like the job, but I did what I was told. Like a soldier. They were afraid of what might happen in the relief camps."

"Men might get together and find they had common interests. The working class might become aware of how they were being used. The proletariat might organize to get power. That's what they were afraid of."

"I'm not a Communist," Malcolm said. "I don't see any point in it. Every man has to find his own way."

Petroff drank down his whisky.

"Petit-bourgeois shit," he said. His face was flushed with anger, and his eyes were bright.

Malcolm was uncomfortable facing Petroff's accusations. He hadn't liked the undercover job. Many of the men seemed like decent guys, and he understood some of their anger, being treated like criminals because they were unemployed. It wasn't what he'd imagined doing when he'd joined the RCMP, but he felt a sense of loyalty to the Force, and a fear too, that he could become one of these unemployed, desperate men. He'd done the job.

"We all do what we have to do," he said to Petroff.

Petroff stood up.

"Maybe," he said, "they will send you and me out to-
gether. And maybe what I will have to do is kill you because
I know you can't be trusted."

He turned and walked past the bar and out the pub door.
The woman at the bar glanced toward Malcolm and then
away. He wondered what she saw on his face.

15

Borden sat in the corner of the bar and waited for Tamblyn to arrive. He'd already decided that he didn't want to talk here, not when it was this important. He'd brought his car and parked it nearby. It would be easier, he thought, to keep in control of the conversation if he was behind the wheel of his own car. The driver is always in control. In the driver's seat. He just had to extend the investigation a little farther, and there was a jackpot for him, he knew that. He could sense it there, waiting. All the circumstances seemed to have conspired in his favour.

He saw Tamblyn at the door, waited, still, until Tamblyn spotted him, and then waited again, not watching the man approach the table. No sooner had Tamblyn sat down than the waiter was beside him.

"Rye and water," Tamblyn said. "Another for you?"

"No. I'm fine."

The waiter vanished and Tamblyn looked toward him, smiling and friendly.

"How are things? It's been a while."

"Not that long."

"Is it going well for you, Borden?"

"Yes, it is."

The waiter arrived with the drink. Tamblyn thanked him, with a kind of friendly sincerity, as if he had done them a special favour. Tamblyn took a sip.

"Bud's been asking after you," he said.

"I have my car here," Borden said. "After you finish your drink, let's take a drive."

"We can talk here."

"I'd rather talk in the car."

"Suit yourself," Tamblyn said. He sat back in his chair, relaxed and jovial.

"You know what my daughter said to me this morning? She said why doesn't the United States have a leaf on their flag? She thinks it's great, the maple leaf. Though I think she might like a flower even better."

"Tell her about the Quebec flag. That has a flower on it."

"That's right, Borden. A lily, isn't it? Didn't think of that. I'll mention it to her tonight when I get home. Make her even more disappointed in the old Stars and Stripes."

"I imagine any daughter of yours would be pretty loyal to her country."

"Deep down, sure, but Canada's different, not like countries where they have to go to special American schools. Here they're just like all the other kids. It's good for them."

Borden finished his drink and called the waiter

over, handed him enough to pay for the two drinks with a good tip.

"Why don't you let me get it?" Tamblyn said.

"My turn."

Tamblyn sipped his drink.

"You seem very edgy tonight, Borden."

Borden just shrugged. He didn't like to think that he was giving anything away.

"How are things with your girl?" Tamblyn said.

"They aren't," Borden said, "not right now."

"You need it, you know, Borden. Good for your health."

"There's lots of time for that."

Tamblyn was looking straight at him.

"You look like a hound-dog with the scent of coon in his mouth," Tamblyn said. "Like you just can't wait to start tearing the fur off him."

Borden laughed.

"I guess I shouldn't have skipped lunch," he said. They stood up from the table and made their way out. Borden led the way to his car and opened the passenger door for Tamblyn.

"Good service you people give," Tamblyn said.

Borden started the car. He drove out toward the suburbs. Cars flashed past. A few flakes of snow skidded over the windshield.

"What is it you want?" Tamblyn said.

Borden drove past the university and pulled off into a suburban street lined with trees. He pulled the car over to the curb and shut off the engine.

"I've got something big," Borden said.

"Tell me about it."

"Not yet."

"Then why are we here?"

"You said you might be able to be helpful."

"That's right. Bud suggested that I try to ease things for you if that was possible."

Borden looked at the man, the straight nose and strong chin, and old-fashioned moustache. No matter how he tried to work it, Borden was doing the asking. He was the suitor fearing rejection.

"If I needed some help, how would we proceed?"

"Depends what you need," Tamblyn said.

"Watchers."

"In town here?"

"No."

"You can't use your own people?"

"Right now we don't have any people. I can't use RCMP people."

"Why not?"

"I can't tell you that," Borden said.

"You have to give me something."

"You can trust me."

"I can't do anything on my own. I'd need clearance."

"How would we get that?"

"You give me a memo on the investigation so far. An outline of what you've found and what you think it's leading to. You shoot that over to me, and I can probably clear it with Hurnick and Fedor."

"I hope you're kidding," Borden said.

"Why?"

"Even talking to you could get me thrown out. Chasing this case on my own could get me put in jail if it goes the wrong way. You can't expect me to give you a written report on what I'm doing."

"I've got to have something," Tamblyn said.

Borden sat in silence. He'd known how hard this was going to be, but he'd told himself he had to go through with it. What he was doing was, in the long run, what he'd been hired to do. There was an undiscovered agent, guilty in the past, probably guilty in the present. McAllister had missed him, and Borden had found him. The Americans had probably wanted only to make a connection with Borden, to set him up as one of their good friends, to suggest that they thought he was worth helping out. Nothing was supposed to come of it except a close relationship with Hurnick, with Tamblyn, something they might use later on, something to get him on their side.

"I don't think Hurnick expected me to find anything," Borden said, "but I have. It was there waiting to be found, and I got it. I could blow the whistle now, but it will work better if I have more. With you or without."

"Give me a bit of help," Tamblyn said. "You've got an active agent, is that it?"

"I think so. I've got the past connection. I don't think there's any chance I could be wrong. Nobody's touched him."

"You want to know if he's still active."

"It makes a big difference."

"If he's not, this could waste a lot of our money."

"You're willing to do it?"

"I didn't say that."

"I need to know."

"Maybe you should talk to him, see if you can shake him up."

"I talked to him yesterday. I'd like to have watchers

there right now. I told him I was a journalist. The questions I was asking were all legitimate. If there's nothing going on, he'll ignore it. If there is something happening, he's going to make a move. Soon."

"You not only want help, you want it right away."

"It's no use to me later."

Tamblyn looked toward him and smiled. It was a professional smile, as if he were one of the actors he resembled.

"You're asking a hell of a lot."

"You can do it if you want."

"They'd have to report to me," Tamblyn said.

"I have to accept that."

"We can't afford to leave them on forever."

"A couple of weeks would tell a lot. It would help to have a tap on his phone, but that's not possible."

"Maybe you should take them the story now. Tell them what you've got."

"They'd tell me it's all in the past. That it doesn't matter any more. I have to prove it's still alive."

Tamblyn looked ahead down the street. A young couple was walking toward them. The boy had his arm around the girl.

"You're asking a hell of a lot," Tamblyn said.

16

Margaret had made the decision in bed the night before. Listening to the rattle of the freezing rain that was falling against the window, worrying about all the things that might go wrong with the house — the power was sure to be off for a while, and the old furnace might not come back on afterward — hating the solitude that kept her lying stiff and afraid, she decided, as she should have years before, to empty out her mother's room and her father's, and to try to rent them. There weren't a lot of people looking for single rooms in town, but she might find one or two. It would mean she would have to keep the furnace turned higher, which would cost her more for oil, but the rent would take care of that.

Margaret had lain awake for a long time last night. Partly it was the noise of the rain. She knew that it was freezing and treacherous outside, and although she didn't drive, dangerous weather always made her nervous, as if she were waiting for someone who was on the road, struggling toward her. There was, she knew, no one coming over the bad roads to this house, but still, the weather frightened her.

Once she had made her decision, it was different. She had felt warmer, comforted. She had allowed herself to think of pleasant possibilities. She made lists of the sort of people who might rent her rooms, an older man whose wife had died, but who was in good health and pleasant to talk to. A young man, just come to town to work and wanting to stay with her for a few months until he knew how long he'd be settled here. Or a girl who'd got in trouble and couldn't stay with her family. Margaret had dwelt long on that possibility until she could see the girl in her mind, the awkwardness with which she moved when she was close to her time. She might even bring the baby back to the house. They could raise it to-gether — oh, she knew that was impossible, but she allowed herself to imagine it. She indulged herself. She was, at least, making a change; something new could happen. Margaret knew that it might be small, be ordinary, but she let herself hope for something more, now she had started to hope. She had always distrusted hope, been afraid that it would lead her into danger, a danger that she couldn't somehow define.

Warmed by the thought of new possibilities, she had fallen asleep and this morning wakened to see the sunlight glittering on the trees coated with ice. A shining branch tapped against the window of her father's room where she had decided to begin. On the bed lay his clerical vestments. She had disposed of a lot of his clothes after his death, the ordinary things, but his clerical collar and vestments had remained in the closet, as if his ghost might need them to prove that he had been ordained, that he was a man of God. Well, he was long enough gone now that he had been tried and proved, and no human spirit seemed to reside in the garments that she had piled there. And no Holy Spirit either. They were just rags. But even at that, she didn't know quite how to dispose of them. She felt as if they, like an empty church, ought to be deconsecrated before being turned to other uses. Perhaps it was simplest just to bundle them and throw them out; it had more dignity than seeing them go to a second-hand store where someone would buy them to wear on Hallowe'en.

She wondered if her father had ever let himself know that his ordination was a mistake, no, perhaps not his ordination, but his attempt to live as a parish clergyman. His life in the First War as a regimental chaplain had been some kind of high point. Perhaps, in the face of all that death, he was able to summon up an intensity of belief that was lacking in the day-to-day life of a parish. Or maybe she had got him wrong. Perhaps the lack of faith was hers. Perhaps he didn't use words beyond the expected, the conventional, because for him those words were full of meaning, and it was his daughter who lacked the ears to hear.

If that was so, what was she to make of her mother's illness, her own sense of a secret that haunted the house? The young chaplain had come back from war. A year later, he had married, and a year after that, his first daughter was born, and that daughter had no memories that weren't of a house oppressed. Was it only the simple fact of an unhappy marriage? If it was that, how did her father accommodate his beliefs to the facts of his life? Was the hollowness she heard in his professions the echo of the fact that he couldn't accommodate belief and fact? He was, in later life, a selfish man, who expected Margaret to fit herself to his convenience, but now and then he would talk about his chaplaincy in the war, and Margaret thought she could imagine a different man, unselfish, courageous, even gay. If she had never married, it was partly that her life had been demanded by this house, by her sick mother, then her aging father, but partly too because she could see marriage only as a wounding, a decline from gaiety to stoic endurance. Her father had behaved well, or at least politely, with what he saw as kindness.

Malcolm had made her see marriage differently. Not that he spoke much of Jean; very seldom in fact. But the pain that he endured was the pain of loss, and one could feel from him a kind of warmth, fulfilment. Margaret had hardly ever seen him and Jean together. Once or twice on the street, she thought, and yet Jean's presence was with him wherever he went.

It was Malcolm's kindness and strength that had made Margaret able to plan a future different from the past.

The ice-covered branch knocked against the window again, as if summoning her, and as she looked out, she saw Malcolm's car pull up in front of the church. He climbed out, walking with care across the icy pavement, and made his way to the door of the Sunday school, where he took out his keys and let himself in. Just after he had gone in another car, black and new-looking, drove past the church, slowly. It stopped half a block up the road and sat there with the engine running, white steam puffing from the exhaust pipe into the freezing air. It was a strange car and had no business here. They, whoever they were, were watching Malcolm again, pursuing him somehow, and she was about to go out and confront the driver when the car pulled away and vanished.

How did it fit, this car that was watching him? Margaret felt that she understood his life, its dignity, the love for Jean, but there must be something more, something that she couldn't know and understand. She turned back to the room, opened the bottom drawer of the chest and took out the pile of black notebooks that contained her father's sermons, notes neatly written and numbered, scriptural references accurately documented. She set them on the bed beside the vestments. She opened one. *The gift of grace,* said a note at the top of the page. Beneath was a citation to one of Paul's letters. She closed the book. The words, the handwriting, seemed to take a cold grip on her heart, as if to stifle the foolish childish hope that she had been feeling.

She found her coat and boots and started across the street to the church. Once or twice she nearly lost her footing, and her pace, she thought, must be absurd and awkward, little steps to avoid slipping. There was sand and salt on the road, but even so, patches were still icy and treacherous.

Margaret went in the Sunday school door, which Malcolm had left open. She could hear the vacuum in the basement, but she didn't allow herself to go down yet. First she went into the church and knelt. She

tried to pray, but all she could think of was the handwriting in her father's books of sermons; his presence
stifled prayer.

She made her way back to the basement. When
Malcolm saw her coming he switched off the vacuum.

"I would have put sand on the walk if I'd known
you were coming over," he said.

"I took baby steps," she said.

"I had trouble getting the car out of my drive."

Margaret wondered whether to tell him about the
black car, the man watching him. She would tell him
her good news instead.

"I've decided to empty out those other two bed-
rooms," she said. "Try to see if I can rent them."

"That's a good idea."

"If I have a little company, it should keep me from
going senile quite as fast."

"Do you need any help?" he said. "Moving things?"

"I don't think so. Not yet. So far I've just started to
pile up things I should throw out. I haven't quite
managed to put anything in the garbage yet."

"Do you have a lot stored in there?" he said.

"Not all that much really. It only seems a lot when
you try to decide how to dispose of it."

They were silent now. There was nothing more
that needed to be said, and he was ready to go back to
his work. It was time for Margaret to go, but she hesitated. Malcolm was looking toward her, and there
was something in his eyes that was sad and worried.
Again she wanted to tell him about the car, but again
she hesitated. Perhaps it was only her fantasy, a matter of trying to make herself important to him. It

seemed like a kind of intrusion on his privacy. She turned away.

"I'd best get back to it," she said.

"Let me know if you need help," Malcolm said and turned on the vacuum.

Margaret made her way back up the stairs, and returned to the church. She knelt, and now she could pray, though the prayer was wordless, and she could not tell if she was praying for Malcolm, for herself, or for the whole of God's world. It hardly seemed to matter.

A few minutes later, she rose from her knees and left the church. Sunlight was reflected from the ice on every branch and twig and the street was like some gigantic diamond shop.

When Margaret got back to her house, she searched for some plastic garbage bags she thought she had. The next thing, if she was going to have people in the house, would be to put some kind of order in the kitchen, empty the drawers and decide what to keep and what to throw out. She finally found the garbage bags in a bin with some onions, and she took them up the stairs, piled the vestments into one of them and sealed it with a twist tie. She would feel self-conscious about putting it out for the garbage men, as if Rhoda Maynard who lived across the way might know what was inside and spread it all over town. Still, it must be done. She began to put the notebooks into another bag, but they were heavy, and she was afraid the bag would break and spill them across the lawn. That would be too much.

What she needed was a box. She thought perhaps there was one in the back shed, and she went down the stairs to look. It was just as she was going past the kitchen window that she saw the black car again. It was parked down near the corner. Margaret couldn't see the licence number from here. For a moment she stood at the window, her eyes on the car, as if she could see into it, see the man inside, see into his mind and know what he was doing, why he was pursuing Malcolm. But all she saw was the shine of the windshield reflecting sunlight, and behind it the hint of a dark shape. Margaret stood behind one window watching him, as behind another he waited for Malcolm. She must do something, but she didn't know what. Across the road, she saw the heavy figure of Rhoda Maynard appear and scatter some salt on the steps outside her house. She vanished back inside. Margaret had not moved. The dark form was still there in the car.

Margaret walked to the door, took her coat from the rack and pulled it on. She would confront the man, ask who he was and demand that he leave Malcolm alone. Not that he would be frightened of Margaret. Perhaps she would only take down the licence number and report him to the police.

What if he was from the police? Impossible, that the police should be watching Malcolm. He was a good man.

Margaret crossed the lawn, where the long blades of grass were like dark spikes rising from a white bed of ice crystals. It was easier to walk here, and she moved quickly, her eye on the car. As she got close to the street, she saw the man inside move as if he had seen her. She walked more quickly.

The engine of the car had started, and it began to

move. Margaret waved to the man to stop him, but he ignored her and the black body of the car, the chrome shining like the ice on the trees, was going to pass and vanish. She waved and tried to shout, but no sound seemed to come; she was frightened as in a dream. She must reach the car, to stop him, to prevent him from troubling Malcolm again; she ran into the road, her arms waving. For a moment it was as if she were back in her house, at the window, watching this ridiculous figure in a flapping coat, racing into the path of a moving car. Her feet slipped and she was out of control, aware that she was close to the wheels, then only knowing that the little figure in the road was hurt and falling.

17

Across the table from him, Beaudry was smiling broadly, but to Borden the smile seemed a mockery, as if the man knew that Borden might be in trouble and was laughing at him.

"Well," Borden said, in answer to a quip of Beaudry's, "nobody ever called the Mounties subtle."

"The subtlety of a goddam moose," Beaudry said. "A northern *Alberta* moose," he said and laughed again.

Beaudry was having a good time. He seemed to like Borden, but Borden couldn't really take it as reassuring, not yet. It was going to be a long time before he stopped seeing the knife behind every smile.

"I'm not in a subtle ministry," Borden said.

Beaudry liked that.

"No," he said. "Between the Mounties and the goddam prison system, it's not too subtle at all."

"Not like your medieval theologians working on the law of the sea."

"That's right," Beaudry said. "How many codfish can dance on an imaginary boundary?"

"Sometimes," Borden said, "I think I could stand a little subtlety."

"Want me to give you a job?" Beaudry said.

"It's a thought."

"I figured you'd want to finish up the new legislation. Take the credit and then get out."

"If there is any credit."

"Somebody will know. Sure, they'll jump all over you in Parliament, but they're always gonna do that."

Borden looked at the man opposite him, the mobile features and the cold grey eyes. Did Beaudry know more than he let on?

"I don't really care," he said, "whether I'm there to the end or not."

"You think you'd like to work in Justice?" Beaudry said.

Borden didn't want to seem too eager.

"Could be."

"You're like a young girl, Borden. *Peut-être oui, peut-être non.*"

"Of course I'd like to work in Justice," Borden said. "If it was a good position."

"In Justice they're all good positions."

Beaudry drained his glass.

"I got to get going," he said. "We'll be in touch."

"Good," Borden said. He watched him go and ordered another drink. He was tempted to get royally drunk. But not here, in public. He should stop on the way home for a bottle of whisky and go to bed with it. When the waiter brought his new drink, Borden sipped it and surveyed the room. A couple of men were leaning across the piano toward the woman whose fingers moved automatically over the keys. In a corner, two young women, both dressed in suits, talked intensely. A man and woman in their sixties sat silently across from each other, their eyes not meeting.

There it was, there was the world. It didn't interest him much.

As he turned to the doorway, he saw Cynthia. Standing at the door. It was how long, two months, three, since he'd seen her? She was wearing a pleated skirt of dark blue, and a pale-blue sweater. Her face was bright from the cold outside. She looked around the bar, and when she saw Borden she didn't react. Just looked at him. He couldn't tell what was in her mind. He smiled and nodded, and she walked to his table. She was perfect, somehow, like an illustration from a magazine, like a mannequin.

"Are you meeting someone?" he said.

"No. I just dropped in for a drink."

"Why don't you sit down?"

"Are you waiting for someone?"

"No. The guy I was drinking with just left."

She sat.

"Disgraceful, isn't it?" she said, "me coming to bars alone."

"Do you do it often?"

"This is the first time. I don't know why. I just didn't want to go home and cook my dinner yet."

"You could phone someone."

"No," she said. "I couldn't."

She wouldn't meet his eyes.

"You're not with him."

"It didn't work out."

Borden waved to the waiter and ordered Cynthia a drink. Dubonnet on ice with lemon; it was what she always drank in public, though at home she would drink beer or whisky if he did. Odd, how he was thinking about that as if they were still together.

"So what happened?" he said.

"I don't really want to talk about it, Borden. It just didn't work out."

"When did you break up?"

"A couple of weeks ago."

She had come to the bar looking for him; he knew that now. He looked at her pretty face, and their eyes met.

"How are you?" she said.

"Not bad. I'm thinking of changing jobs."

"Why?"

"It's pretty boring where I am. I think I could find something better."

"I thought you liked it."

"I did for a while."

Borden wanted to touch her, but he wasn't sure how she'd respond. Better to wait.

"I was here with a guy from Justice," he said. "It sounds like he'd offer me a job."

"That's a good sign, isn't it?"

"Yeah, I think it is."

She picked up her drink.

"You're still just as pretty," he said.

She smiled and then looked away.

"Glad you think so," she said.

"We could go out for dinner."

"That would be nice."

Borden looked around the bar. It seemed like a

different place now. The older man and woman were talking to each other, laughing. Borden looked back at Cynthia, pleased and excited by her beauty, the bright blue eyes with their long, perfect lashes. He'd always liked to be seen in public with her.

As he finished his drink, he thought over the conversation with Beaudry. Perhaps he could avoid the mess that had seemed to be about to engulf him. Cynthia's arrival, her desire to be with him, was a sign.

"How about Mamma Teresa's?" he said on the way out of the bar.

"Wouldn't that be bad luck?" she said. "It's the last place we went to."

"All the more reason to go there."

When he helped her on with her coat, he let his hands rest on her shoulders, and she stood still, not moving away. It was exciting to touch her. He'd been alone too much, a couple of one-night stands the only break in the isolation. Tonight Cynthia would share his bed, and he'd forget about Tamblyn and Fraser and Petroff, and just be aware of the warmth of her body.

As they sat at dinner, he stroked the back of her hand with his fingers, and liked the way it made her smile.

"You came to the bar looking for me, didn't you?" he said.

She didn't answer.

"Didn't you?"

She shrugged.

"It's the only bar I ever go to," he said.

She took up her wineglass and drank from it. She
wouldn't look at him.

"Why won't you answer?" he said.

"You make me feel stupid."

"No. I just wanted to know."

"Well, I guess I did. I came looking for you."

He took her hand.

"I'm glad I was there. I don't go very often."

"Maybe I knew you were there."

"You mean you saw me."

"No, just that I knew."

Borden drank his wine. His body was hot and
roused, hungry to touch her skin. The light in the
restaurant seemed to thicken and darken. He
squeezed her hand.

"Let's go," he said.

"Where?"

"To my place."

"I'm not sure. Tonight."

"Of course," he said. "Tonight. Now."

"I'm not sure."

He called for the bill, got them out and led her
along the street to his apartment building. In the ele-
vator, he kissed her, and her mouth was soft and
open, but when he drew back, there were tears in her
eyes.

"It feels good," he said. "It's been too long."

She shrugged and wouldn't look at him. He put his
arm around her and took her down the hall. As he
unlocked the apartment door, she stood back from
him, looking young and shy. They stepped into the
darkness, and he pulled her body against his.

18

His feet were cold as he walked across the snow, and the cold was moving upward into the rest of his body. By the time he reached his car, he was shivering uncontrollably. He stopped by the car, and looked back across the snowy ground to the place, beside two existing gravestones, where Margaret's body had been put. There had been a respectable gathering of people at the church for the funeral, mostly local people with church connections, but few had come to the cemetery. Malcolm had followed the black hearse here, and now he turned to look back. He rememberd the optimism she had felt the last time he'd seen her.

Malcolm got in the car and started for home. The grey light of the day reflected his bitterness. The piles of dirty snow by the side of the road, pimpled with gravel, were the mirror of his state of mind. He drove carelessly, angrily, but much of the anger was against himself, that somehow he had drawn Margaret to her death. He had tempted her into a world where men drove without caring who they ran down.

When Malcolm reached his house, there was a car waiting in the drive, the engine running to keep its occupant warm in the winter day. Malcolm wasn't surprised to see it. Someone always came with some excuse, some explanation.

He pulled up beside the house. The drive from the cemetery hadn't been long enough to heat the car, and his feet were even colder now. He'd loaded the stove with wood before he left; the house would be comfortable. What old age left you was the simple bodily demands. You wanted your feet to be warm.

As he got out of the car and walked toward the house, he didn't look toward the other car, but he heard its engine turned off, the door open and shut. As he pulled out his keys and opened the lock, he heard footsteps on the snow behind him. He turned as he opened the door. The tall bulky figure of Tom McAllister. Malcolm held the door open for him, and the two of them entered the small house.

It was warm, but not as hot as Malcolm had hoped. Why could he think of nothing but getting heat into his bones? To prove to himself that he was alive, perhaps, that he was not lying on the frozen earth with Margaret. He went to the stove, put on more wood and opened the drafts.

Tom McAllister had taken off his coat and settled on the couch. Malcolm turned back toward him.

"Can I get you something? Tea? Coffee? Whisky?"

"Whisky. It's early, but I could stand a drink."

"Help you through a difficult situation."

"Not that difficult."

"It should be."

"Why?"

Malcolm went to a cupboard and took out the bottle of whisky. He poured some into two glasses and handed one to McAllister.

"Was it your Mr De Vries that killed her, or someone else?" Malcolm said.

"I told you before. I don't know any De Vries."

"You told me. I didn't have to believe it."

"I don't have to believe you either."

"A different situation. I'm on the outside. No secrets."

"If you didn't have any secrets, that Russian wouldn't have been knocking on your door."

"I suppose."

"Why did they come back after all those years?"

"You'd be more likely to know that than I would."

"You're sure they left you alone all that time?"

"That's what I told you."

"They don't usually let people off the hook."

"Once I'd left the Force, I had nothing to offer. When I said no, I was pretty firm."

"How was that?"

"It was when we first moved to the country. I put a couple of bullet holes in their car. They seemed to take that seriously."

McAllister sipped the whisky.

"Why did you do that?"

"I didn't like them or the way they operated. I did someone a favour and they used it to blackmail me. I didn't want to leave the Force, but it was the only way to get free. We'd left Ottawa. Jean was pregnant. I told them to leave me alone. I would have killed one of them if they hadn't."

"So why did you listen to the one who came this time?"

"Curiosity. Maybe a little greed. He was offering money."

"Were you going to take it?"

"I hadn't made up my mind."

"That means you were."

"I needed the money. I was tempted. Then your Mr De Vries turned up."

"And you called me."

Malcolm looked at the large figure on the couch. There was something shapeless, undefined, about him, as if he had suddenly grown out of his clothes at adolescence and never come to be at ease with his own size. His big hands hung between his legs, loosely clasped. He looked as if he might be slow of thought, ponderous, though Malcolm knew that was an illusion.

"Was he one of yours?" Malcolm said. "The man who ran her down?"

"I don't know that he was one of anybody's. It may have been a simple hit and run."

"I'm sure Rhoda Maynard told you the same thing she told me. She hasn't the imagination to make anything up. She said Margaret was waving at the man in the car, trying to stop him. Margaret had her eccentricities, but she was no fool. Whoever it was, he was up to something, probably surveillance. Of me."

"He wasn't working for me."

"I don't believe you," Malcolm said.

"It's the truth."

"Who else could it be? The Russians have no reason to have surveillance on me, and probably no resources to do it."

"Don't underrate their resources."

"It doesn't make sense that they'd be watching me."

"It makes sense that they wouldn't want to be caught at it. That they wouldn't stop after an accident."

"Maybe," Malcolm said, but the shape of that story was wrong. McAllister was staring down at his hands.

"There's more to this, isn't there?" Malcolm said. "There's some part of it you're not telling me."

"You know there are lots of things I can't tell you."

"But this isn't just official secrets. You've got something under your skin. You look like a man who's made a mistake."

McAllister looked up at him.

"You're in no damned position to make accusations. You were a member of the RCMP and you betrayed your trust. You betrayed the Force and you betrayed your country. And I think you were ready to do it again."

"The first time was a long time ago. I had my reasons, good or bad. This time, I don't know. I guess I was playing with the idea. I needed the money."

"Why would you need the money?"

Malcolm looked at the man. He'd never known him well, and it was years since he'd known him at all, but he had to tell him the truth.

"My son ran away from his wife and family. I'd like to do something for them, and I don't have much to do it with."

"Why did he run away?"

"I don't know. He was always . . . a little distant. Jean would have understood. She was better at things like that."

McAllister had looked sharply away the moment Jean's name was mentioned.

"You never forgave her, did you?" Malcolm said, "For choosing me."

"I never forgave you for taking her."

"I loved her."

"So did I," McAllister said. He drank the whisky, fast, as if to burn his throat, punish himself. "You ruined my life," he said.

"There were other women."

"Not for me."

Malcolm took the bottle to McAllister and poured his glass full.

"We were happy, Tom," he said. "Since she died, I don't care much about anything, except maybe my grandchildren, and I hardly know them. And Margaret. She was a kind woman. I'd like to see something done about the man who killed her."

"Revenge."

"That's right."

McAllister drank more of the whisky.

"I just had time to know Jean was the woman I wanted to marry when you took her away."

Malcolm poured himself more whisky.

"I think one of the reasons I never thought of you as the one who warned Petroff," McAllister said, "is that I couldn't bear to think of you at all. I should have known."

"I spent years waiting for someone to knock on the door."

"Did you tell Jean?"

"Not at the time. Later."

McAllister looked back at him, angry again.

"And she accepted that?"

"Yes."

There was a heavy, turgid silence. Malcolm listened to the wind in the stove-pipes.

"Is Petroff really dead?" he said.

"That's what they tell me," McAllister said.

Malcolm studied the other man. There was something wrong, something out of place. There was part of the story that he wasn't getting. Probably he'd never know. The room seemed full of distrust, a thick strangling medium he couldn't breathe. Maybe McAllister was finally going to get his revenge.

"Are you going to pull something on me?" Malcolm said. "Say the deal's off, and I'll be charged for what happened thirty years ago."

"No."

The silence after the word was heavy, ominous.

"Do I still go along with the Russians if they call?"

"We'll see. It might be better to cut it off. I could see that your contact is sent back where he came from."

"Why don't you want to go on with it?"

"I don't know if I do or don't. But I think there may be enough mess already."

"Don't you have to consult anybody? You sound as if you're making all the decisions."

"I'm making the ones that count," McAllister said. He stood up. "I'll let you know," he said.

He pulled on his coat and made his way out. He didn't say goodbye. As he went out, cold air came in through the open doorway, and Malcolm shivered. He stood close to the stove, listened as McAllister's car started and drove away. Malcolm was helpless now. He was in the hands of others, and he didn't like the feeling. The chill still wouldn't leave him, as if he'd caught something at the cemetery, some new and fierce kind of frost that had settled far down in his body and would never leave again.

He went to the kitchen to put on the kettle. He'd make scalding tea. He'd burn out the ice that was in his blood.

On the table was a letter from Connie, thanking him for the last money he'd sent, telling him the news. He regretted that he didn't have anything more to send her.

19

McAllister had been restless all morning. A man under control, that's what he'd always been, able to discipline himself, to keep things in order, but today he'd walked foolishly around his office, unable to concentrate, studying his watch every few minutes. He'd gone out for an early lunch and come back quickly. There were too many unknowns. He wanted to get it over. If there was going to be a disaster, let it occur.

It must be old age, his nerves going like this. He checked his watch once more. Time to go. He put on a coat and scarf, walked to the door.

He stopped at the door of his office, observed Crawford's quick fingers flicking the keys of the electric typewriter. The machine hummed softly and the letters snapped forward with a rattling sound. The hairline at the back of Crawford's head was sharply delineated. Whoever cut it, shaved it to a precise edge. Crawford had a wife somewhere and children, but McAllister had never met them.

As McAllister watched, the telephone rang. Crawford flicked off the switch of the typewriter and
reached toward the phone in a single gesture. His
conversation once he had answered was economical
almost to the point of being brusque. It gave McAllister satisfaction to watch Crawford at work, everything done the way he would have it. He didn't have
to make polite chatter with Crawford or listen to stories about his private life or be aware of his time of
the month, all the things that would have been compulsory with one of the women secretaries. He and
Crawford understood each other, and that saved a lot
of wasted motion.

McAllister wasn't easy around women. There was
something about them. They were unaccountable.
He'd told himself it was because of Jean, his sense of
betrayal, but he wasn't sure any more if that was the
case. Perhaps it was always in him and that was why
she'd chosen someone else. Fraser: he must have a
weakness for women, involved with this other one
after Jean died. Wanted someone to keep house for
him; it could be that. McAllister found it easier to
have a char come in once a week, someone he never
had to see, just leave the money on the table. No fuss.

"I'll be gone for the afternoon, Crawford," McAllister said and moved away from his position in the
doorway and down the hall. As he moved away, he
wondered if he had looked foolish standing there
watching Crawford work, his mind wandering. Crawford didn't turn, or comment, but he would have noticed; they had an effect, things like that, on what was
thought of you. The word got around that you were

letting things get out of order, and soon enough you were finished.

It might be too late anyway. As he walked toward his car, he considered once again the note he'd found in the mailbox at his house. Just two names. Petroff and Fraser. And a time and place. McAllister checked his watch. It was an hour's drive from here to the meeting-place. The sky was turbulent with clouds that looked as if they would bring snow. McAllister didn't relish driving in the snow. He didn't relish having this meeting at all, and one part of him thought it would be best not to go. It could be six kinds of a trap. But wasn't that what life was, really, when you got down to it? Six kinds of a trap.

Early retirement. It could end up with that. Sent to rot in his little house. It was all right for the others, with wives and children. They could go on trips, move to Florida. McAllister had nothing but his work, and to be deprived of that would be the worst punishment they could find. Bad enough that he'd let himself be tempted into the planning of the new agency, all theory and paperwork. To let himself be pushed out altogether was too much.

He drove through the slow traffic of the city streets, watching, as he always did, for anything that was odd or out of place. An old cop's instincts died hard.

Maybe if they got him out, he'd go back to the prairies. A house on the edge of a small town where he could have a garden and watch the weather coming toward him and passing away. He didn't want to leave and he didn't intend to go easily. Even an old man had a trick or two left up his sleeve.

As he moved through the quick streams of traffic on the Queensway, watching the multitude of anonymous drivers, people he would never meet, he thought of Crawford again, his silent form outside the door of McAllister's private office, always getting everything right. There was a Mrs Crawford; there were little Crawfords. McAllister had never been curious about them before, but now he found himself wondering what they were like. Was the woman pretty? Were the children bright and healthy? Or was it a sad, dreary marriage, silent, laborious? Did Crawford talk about his work? Surely not. He thought of Crawford and Mrs Crawford in bed at night, Crawford telling her about McAllister, perhaps laughing at his peculiarities.

Crawford wouldn't do that.

How was he to know? What had made him think that? It put him on edge, but he couldn't put the idea out of his mind now. He dealt in secrets, betrayals, and yet the simple thought of Crawford's disloyalty could shake him. It was the whole thing with Fraser. The woman's death. Remembering Jean and the past. He wanted to be done with it. Bloody foolishness that he'd left the Russian desk; more bloody foolishness that he hadn't broken young Denny and got rid of him; still more bloody foolishness that he'd left the Force, where he could have put a man like Denny in his place and kept him there.

Why had Denny (if it was Denny — surely it was) set up this meeting out in the country? Why not just come into his office and say what he had to say? Too damn clever. McAllister would see him out on his ear, if he had a chance. When he'd learned about the

woman's death, McAllister had suggested to the police that they have a look at Denny's car on the quiet,
but there had been no signs of a recent accident or
repairs. It had been done carefully and Denny was
none the wiser about it; McAllister had to give him
credit for having the brains not to use his own car,
and to do a fair job of concealing the one he'd used.
If it was Denny.

Was it someone else who'd killed her? Or could it
be that it had no significance? That it was just some
drunken fool behind the wheel on an icy day? The
one witness was that stupid self-important fat
woman, Rhoda something. Maynard.

"She just crumpled right up," the woman kept repeating, "and I said to myself, my God she's dead,
Margaret's dead." She wouldn't be budged on her
statement that this Margaret woman had been running toward the car, waving at the driver, trying to
stop him, and that he had refused to slow down, had
turned, then braked and slid, hitting the thin body.

"There wasn't much to her," the Maynard woman
said. "Skin and bones. She just crumpled right up
and I said to myself, my God she's dead, Margaret's
dead."

Well, and so she was, dead, and nothing would
bring her back. Fraser wanted some kind of revenge,
and McAllister? He wanted to get it all back under
control, wanted to stitch up some of those loose
threads that were threatening to tear apart his life.

The first snowflakes had begun to fall, and now
with every minute the air grew thicker with them.
McAllister stepped on the gas, in a hurry to be off the

Queensway before the surface got slippery and someone drove into him.

Once off the Queensway, the route he was planning to take wasn't the shortest one, but it had on it a
couple of places where he could check to see if he was
being watched. He wasn't sure who might be
watching him, but the precaution was habitual and
worth the extra trouble.

The dim landscape of dirty snow was becoming invisible in the whirl of heavy flakes. In another hour
the driving would be perilous, but he had sand and a
shovel in the trunk. He would get to the meeting, and
if he didn't want to make the drive back there would
be a motel nearby that he could stay in.

A night in a bare motel room might be useful for
thinking things out. Once he knew what was to be
thought about.

He passed a junction of three roads and shortly beyond came round a sudden curve and pulled off into
a lane. He waited, watching through the veil of snow
for a car to pass.

He waited five minutes, but no one drove past. He
wasn't being followed. He turned back to the corner
and took a new direction. If they had enough watchers, they might be waiting for him ahead, but that
was unlikely. It would take a huge team in this countryside, unless they knew his destination.

If they knew that, they didn't need watchers.

The road was heavy with snow, and he could feel
the weight of it through the steering. There was a
truck in front of him, going too slowly, but he wasn't
prepared to pass it with visibility as limited as it was.

He drove steadily, mechanically on, following the

truck until it slowed and turned away toward a farm that was only just visible through what was becoming a blizzard. Even now, he felt confident that he could make his way safely through the snow.

By the time he reached the town that was his destination, he thought perhaps the snow was easing a little. He drove down the main street, seeing a bundled-up woman move from a car to the doorway of a grocery store, the face of a man watching the street from inside a lighted window. All the lights were on in the buildings, and they made him feel he would like to be inside, warm, at work on something that challenged his best powers.

At the end of the main street, McAllister made a left turn. His wheels, which had been following the tracks of previous cars, hit the untracked snow of the park where the meeting was supposed to take place, and the car slowed with the resistance, the back wheels sliding a little. He stepped on the gas and forced the car down the park road and into position on the parking-lot beside the river. This was the place the note had directed him to, and now he looked around him for any sign of someone here to meet him. The park was empty. He stared through the windshield, which was beginning to blur whitely, toward the dark, turbulent surface of the river, where thousands of flakes dropped and vanished. He heard no sound but his own breathing. He opened the car door and stepped out where he could hear the menacing mumble of the water. The air was cold on his face, and he thought that a man could be murdered here, his body dumped in the river, the car left somewhere miles away.

Damn nerves. He wasn't used to that kind of thing. Like worrying about what Crawford said about him at home. He got back in the car and turned on the engine to warm it, opened the window on the passenger side so a little air got in. Not to asphyxiate himself. He turned on the windshield wipers, which opened two arcs of darkness in the white curtain. He stared at the river and waited.

The passenger door opened and the man got it.

"McAllister?" the man said.

"That's right."

McAllister looked toward him. The face with its small moustache looked familiar, like some movie actor. McAllister didn't go to movies. The face was handsome, well groomed.

"And you?" he said.

"Burgess."

"Not *Guy* Burgess?"

The man smiled. He had expensive teeth.

"No, sir."

The accent was American. McAllister couldn't tell where from, he was no expert. Had Denny sent this man? No, this Burgess, whoever he really was, didn't take orders from Borden Denny. McAllister watched the face. There was still the trace of a smile.

"Say your piece," he said.

"Malcolm Fraser is the man who tipped off Petroff in 1945 and allowed him to escape. He was a Russian agent. Probably still is."

"How would you know that?"

"They'd known each other from the thirties, a relief camp. They were sent into Europe together in the Second War. Petroff saved Fraser's life. Or Fraser thought he did."

"Proves nothing. Not a damn thing. Wasn't worth the drive to hear that."

The man looked toward McAllister. He wasn't smiling any more.

"It doesn't have to go this way. We could make it friendly and easy."

"Could we?"

"Yes."

"You could, maybe. Not me."

"You have to do everything the hard way."

"Always did."

There was silence except for the mechanical voice of the wipers.

"The proof would be Fraser's confession, and I don't imagine that would be too hard to get. From what I hear, he doesn't seem to care about anything much since his wife died."

"He cared about the woman you killed."

"I killed nobody, Mr McAllister."

"You or Denny, or whoever it was."

"A woman was killed in a car accident."

"Hit and run. She was chasing the man in the car. That might not be an accident."

"I think it was."

"Too late now anyway, I suppose."

"I'd like to see this all sorted out."

"What do you mean by that?" McAllister said.

"I think you know."

The windshield wipers sang quietly. McAllister studied the man beside him. He had small, rather delicate hands. He was shorter than McAllister and thirty pounds lighter. If McAllister wanted to, he could probably kill this man and dump his body in the river. He looked at his own big hands on the steering wheel. Perhaps the man had a gun. It wouldn't surprise him.

McAllister stared at the river, thinking how deep and cold and dangerous it looked. The thoughts that were coming to his mind today startled him. He had thought of killing a man.

"What do you have to offer?" he said.

"Silence. The information about Fraser never gets out."

"Why would I care about that?"

"Because when you reinvestigated, you either failed to discover it, or you discovered it and kept quiet. The second would be the natural assumption."

"Stupidity is the best explanation of most things."

"You think like a cop."

"Right."

"Other people don't. They'd probably assume you had some reason to cover it up. It would be the end of you. They'd put you out to grass."

"They'll soon do that anyway."

"But you don't want to miss the last few years. You've got a great reputation. You'd like to go with that intact, wouldn't you?"

McAllister stared out the window again. It was Malcolm Fraser he should be wanting to kill. He'd taken Jean from him, and he'd got him into this. McAllister wondered how he'd missed Fraser's connection to Petroff. It was so long ago; was it possible to remember now, this long afterward to understand how he had failed to think a necessary thought? The date of Fraser's resignation, the lack of any good reason for it, those things should have set him looking. But they were small things, with no obvious relevance to the job of tracking down Russian spies. It *was* stupidity that had caused him to fail. Or had he preferred to be blind? Certainly he hadn't wanted to think about Fraser and Jean. McAllister stayed in control by putting such complicated, painful matters out of his mind. Once Fraser had left Ottawa, he wished to know nothing of him.

If he'd made the connection, looked at the records, interrogated Fraser, would he have taken the responsibility for putting Jean's husband in jail? Would he have thought that it might destroy their marriage? Too late to think that now. It was all done and vanished.

Yet when Fraser's call had come, saying that he wanted to talk, that it was important, something in McAllister, some knowledge, a suspicion long before put to sleep, had wakened. Fraser's unexpected resignation had come to mind as a fact that must be explained. McAllister had suspected what it all meant.

And hadn't passed it on. He should have called Cliff Slater and given it to the Russian desk, but instead he had driven out to Fraser's place, let him tell his story. And as the words came out, McAllister found that he knew at every moment what to expect, as if he'd heard the story before, and as he listened and analysed, he knew what instinct had told him not to pass it on. *He* was the one who'd missed it, and once he'd realized that, he knew he couldn't ever pass it on, that to admit to this past mistake would destroy him, that he'd have to convince Fraser that he was still active. He'd had to handle it on his own. Once he'd done that, he was trapped, and the trap was one he'd set and sprung himself.

How much of this did Burgess know or guess? Denny, under it all, had some kind of a brain. Between the two of them they might have worked it out. They were offering to let him out of the trap. He didn't need to gnaw off his own leg.

"What do you think of it?" the man said.

"Of what?"

"The deal."

"You offer silence. What do I offer?"

"Silence."

"About what?"

"Everything."

"The accident?"

"It was an accident. It wasn't Denny, you know that, you had his car checked. They'll never find the car or the man, so if you don't stir things up, the case will die a natural death."

"More than can be said for that woman."

"She shouldn't have run in front of a moving car on an icy road."

"Fraser wants something done about it."

"Fraser should be in prison. Tell him so, and tell him to shut his mouth."

"I suppose this could cause you a lot of embarrassment if it came out. Questions in Parliament about American interference in Canadian affairs. Stories in the *New York Times* and the *Washington Post*."

"It won't come out."

"If you convince me."

"It won't come out. You're just insurance. I like to tie down every detail."

McAllister stared again at his own hands. The desire to kill the man was an oddly calm one, something matter of fact. Perhaps killing always seemed like that to the murderer, something abstract and unimportant, yet necessary. Almost a duty. McAllister wondered if he was losing his mind.

"What happens to Denny?" he said. It was Denny that he hated most, more than Fraser, more than this man who sat in his car and insulted him.

"Nothing happens to Denny."

"That's the point of this, I suppose. To protect him."

"In some part."

"You want him to stay right where he is?"

"I don't see why not."

"I see good reasons why not," McAllister said.

The snow had almost stopped. McAllister reached forward and turned off the wipers, his eye was drawn to the hypnotic tumbling of the river. This section would never freeze, even in the coldest weather. There would be bulwarks of ice at the edges, but the fast water would go on.

"What reasons?"

"You own him. We can't have a man at the centre of our security service who owes his career to you."

"But we're on the same side."

McAllister was aware that they were down to the line now. Everything up to here was easy; it didn't matter. But they wanted to keep their man where they had him.

"If we're on the same side, why do you need an ear in our security service?"

"We think Denny's a promising guy."

"Promising . . . promising what to who?"

"We wouldn't want to see his career ruined."

"You have a reputation for protecting your own."

The man didn't answer, but there was a kind of acquiescence in his silence.

"I have a reputation for loyalty myself," McAllister said. "Loyalty to my own people."

"Is that why you covered up for Fraser?"

How far would they go? McAllister wondered. Was there any bluff in them?

"You play poker, Mr Burgess?"

"No. I don't like games."

McAllister tried to think if there was any compromise, any way to avoid betting his whole stake, but he could see none. He might end up sitting alone all day in his house, stoking up on rum and praying for death, but if he did, that was the price he would pay.

"If Denny stays where he is," he said, "there's no deal. No deal of any sort. Nothing to negotiate."

"You've really got it in for him, don't you, McAllister? You want his balls."

"No. I don't like him, not one bit, but that doesn't matter. You're loyal to your people, and I'm loyal to mine. I don't want to see somebody working for us who's owned by you. And if I go along with this deal, you own him, body and soul."

Burgess stroked his moustache slowly with one finger.

"And you're ready to sacrifice your own position."

"There's not much of it left anyway. I made a mistake. They'll let me go quietly. I'll have my pension. It was just a mistake. Stupidity. Stupidity is endless, Burgess. Or whoever you are. Stupidity is endless. Including yours. But yours is something more. You're going to be caught with your fingers in the cookie jar. An international incident. You'll get top marks for enthusiasm, but that's probably not enough, is it?"

The man sat perfectly still, seemed not even to breathe. His profile was sharp, handsome.

"All right, McAllister," he said. "Make me an offer."

"Like what?"

"You're willing to sacrifice yourself to get Denny, is that right?"

McAllister had one more card to play.

"I don't care about Denny. He's not worth it. But I want him out of where he is now."

What he was saying wasn't true. He would have liked to see Denny destroyed, but it wasn't important. Hatred was a kind of self-indulgence.

"If he can arrange a transfer to a good job in another ministry, are you still going to demand your pound of flesh?"

The last card was enough.

"I'll help him pack," he said.

Once again the man was perfectly still, but behind the stillness McAllister could sense a cold anger.

"That's the deal then," the man said sharply. "Denny transfers to something decent with your help. The rest of it never happened. You say nothing. We say nothing. You can let Fraser get away with it."

"All right," McAllister said, "that's the deal."

The man opened the car door and got out. McAllister didn't watch as he walked away. He didn't care where he went. It was late in the afternoon now, and the air was darkening over the dark river. McAllister was tired, but he didn't want to stay the night here. He would drive back to Ottawa and sit down under the blank eyes of the Russian doll, his wooden wife, who, understanding nothing, understood everything.

20

*T*he two men sat in the restaurant booth, one on each side *of the table, and they avoided looking at each other. From behind his back, Malcolm could hear two women and a man talking in slangy French. One of the women laughed. He'd have to get away soon to drive from Montreal to Ottawa in time to get a bit of sleep before work in the morning. He heard the woman's loud laugh again, drained his coffee cup. He checked his watch; Jean would be getting ready for bed. He wanted to be at home, in bed beside her, her arms around him.*

Nick looked toward him, his eyes, in their heavy pouches of skin, dark and strange.

"Why are you warning me?" Nick said.

"Why did you carry me five miles over the mountains?"

"I had my reasons."

"And I have mine."

Nick slurped a mouthful of coffee, wiped his lips.

"Probably your petit-bourgeois conscience. You owe me and you have to pay back."

187

*"Could be." Their eyes met, looked, moved away. "Now
I'm going home to my wife."*

*"You know, Fraser," Nick said, "in another world, I
think we just might have been friends."*

"But this is the one we're in."

"And you're on the wrong side."

"We'll see."

"History's on my side," Nick said.

*Malcolm Fraser looked at the man opposite him, the small
muscular body that had carried his, the way it was crouched,
turned inward, something almost distorted in its wariness,
and yet powerful, dangerous. He knew suddenly how it
would be when they were both dead, as dead as if they'd
never survived to come back from Greece, had never come
down out of those mountains.*

*"History isn't on anybody's side, Nikos," he said, as he
stood up. "Sooner or later, we all get left behind."*

He walked to the door of the restaurant.

21

The car crossed the Burrard Street bridge into downtown Vancouver, drove through a few blocks where the Sunday traffic was light, then turned onto Robson. The sun was shining after a week of rain, and the sidewalks were filled with men and women who had come out to enjoy it, in the hope that perhaps this was the beginning of the early west-coast spring.

When the two of them got out of the car, there was a chill in the air, in spite of the sun. If this was spring, it was coming only slowly and with hesitation. They walked past Lost Lagoon, where an old man was throwing bread to the ducks. There was always an old man there throwing bread to the ducks. One after another, it seemed, these old men came out of houses and high-rises, and trooped down to the park, regular as soldiers, to take their places here with their bags of bread, absolute as icons. When one died, another took his place. The man and the boy took the underpass that led them to the other side of Georgia

Street as it rose through the small forest to the Lion's Gate Bridge. They began to walk on a narrow path through the high redwoods and cedars, the air between the trees damp and clinging, hints even here in these tamed acres of the fearful damp silence of the rain forest.

The boy took the man's hand.

"Can we go to the zoo?" he said.

"Any place you want," the man said.

Through the trees on the right, he could see the masts of the boats at the yacht club. Even in the cold and without sails, they seemed gay, somehow, the masts tilting now and then with a gust of wind. Beyond them the high-rises of the city, hundreds of them, it seemed, glittering in the sun. He wanted to hold the boy's hand tighter, but he was afraid to, it might frighten him. Go slowly, he said to himself. You've got lots of time. You've got all the rest of your life to love this boy and his sister. And they're all you have to love.

At the zoo, they stood for a long time and watched the seals, diving and swimming in their small pool. The boy was a quiet person, and he seemed to carry the fact of his father's absence carefully inside him, like something precious and easily broken.

After the zoo, they followed another footpath along the edge of the water. A heavy-set young man in a purple jogging suit ran past them breathing heavily, and two lovers, a dark man and a short plain woman with a tight worried face, walked past in a concentrated silence, the man's arm around the woman's shoulders. A single-engine Otter rose from the surface of the harbour and seemed to hang in the sunlight for a moment before turning in the air and crossing between them and the mountains to set off up the coast.

In the afternoon sunlight, the mountains were patches of dark and light, snow at the tops glittering brightly. The man couldn't quite get used to the mountains, invisible in rain and fog, and then suddenly appearing over the city, still and angular, snow and trees and bare rock faces. The mountains and the ocean made this the most visual of cities. You were always seeing water or earth, and even the proliferation of high-rises couldn't altogether shut them out.

They were standing in front of the totem poles. The boy turned to him.

"Do you know what it means?" he said, pointing to one of the poles.

"No," he said, "but I'll find out."

He looked at the wild eyes, the geometric designs, the straight wooden wings. The colours were bright and the carved poles towered above the man and the boy.

"Next time we come," he said, "I'll know about them, and I'll tell you. I'll get some books from the library."

The boy stood still, watching the hieratic poles as if they might speak to him.

"Are you going to stay here, Grampa? Until my Dad comes back?"

"Yes," he said. "I'm going to stay here."

He'd found a job of sorts, the previous week, as night cleaner in a restaurant. It was hard work, but he could manage it.

They walked along the side of the water. A ferry was crossing Burrard Inlet to North Vancouver. It looked very bright, white and black on the blue water, like a toy boat riding to toy houses in front of toy mountains. They wandered out onto the beach. The tide was out, and there were peeled cedar logs along the edge of the water, drift logs that had been moved by wind and current and come ashore here.

He was like that, a drift log washed ashore.

"My mum said you were in a war. That you were wounded."

"That's right."

"Did it hurt a lot?"

"Yes, I guess so. It's hard to remember that part now."

"Did you ever think you might die?"

"I was sure I was going to."

"What happened?"

"A man saved my life."

The boy turned to him, the pale eyes, like Jean's he'd noticed recently, thoughtful, his face very serious.

"Really?"

"Yes."

"Do you still know him?"

"I haven't seen him for years. That was a long time ago. I think he's dead now. That's what someone told me."

They walked on in silence, along the edge of the water that spoke gently among the stones. Ahead of them, the path turned into the high dark trees, away from the busy waterway, the ships coming and going, the tiny seaplanes rising into the sun. They would

walk on to the other side of the park where they
could look out across English Bay into Georgia Strait.
There they would see the dark, still forms of ships in
the offing, waiting to come ashore.